CW00669490

Band

Music by
Richard Oberacker

Book & Lyrics by
Robert Taylor & Richard Oberacker

This work is published by Samuel French, an imprint of Concord Theatricals Corp.

No one shall make any changes in this title(s) for the purpose of production. No part of this book may be reproduced, stored in a retrieval system, scanned, uploaded, or transmitted in any form, by any means, now known or yet to be invented, including mechanical, electronic, digital, photocopying, recording, videotaping, or otherwise, without the prior written permission of the publisher. No one shall share this title(s), or any part of this title(s), through any social media or file hosting websites.

For all inquiries regarding motion picture, television, online/digital and other media rights, please contact Concord Theatricals Corp.

THIRD-PARTY MATERIALS USE NOTE

Licensees are solely responsible for obtaining formal written permission from copyright owners to use copyrighted third-party materials (e.g., incidental music not provided in connection with a performance license, artworks, logos) in the performance of this play and are strongly cautioned to do so. If no such permission is obtained by the licensee, then the licensee must use only original materials and materials that the licensee owns and controls. Licensees are solely responsible and liable for clearances of all third-party copyrighted materials, and shall indemnify the copyright owners of the play(s) and their licensing agent, Concord Theatricals Corp., against any costs, expenses, losses and liabilities arising from the use of such copyrighted third-party materials by licensees. For music, please contact the appropriate music licensing authority in your territory for the rights to any incidental music not provided in connection with a performance license.

IMPORTANT BILLING AND CREDIT REQUIREMENTS

If you have obtained performance rights to this title, please refer to your licensing agreement for important billing and credit requirements.

BANDSTAND premiered at the Paper Mill Playhouse in Milburn, New Jersey on October 8, 2015 (Mark S. Hoebee, Producing Artistic Director; Todd Schmidt, Managing Director).

BANDSTAND began previews on Broadway at the Bernard B. Jacob Theatre on March 31, 2017, officially opening April 26, 2017.

BANDSTAND premiered on Broadway at the Bernard B. Jacobs Theatre on April 26, 2017. The production was directed and choreographed by Andy Blankenbuehler, with music direction by Fred Lassen, scenic design by David Korins, costume design by Paloma Young, lighting design by Jeff Croiter, and sound design by Nevin Steinberg. The production stage manager was Mark Dobrow, the stage manager was Julia P. Jones, and the assistant stage manager was Colyn W. Fiendel. The cast was as follows:

JULIA TROJAN	Laura Osnes
DONNY NOVITSKI	Corey Cott
MRS. JUNE ADAMS	Beth Leavel
NICK RADEL	Alex Bender
JOHNNY SIMPSON	Joe Carroll
DAVY ZLATIC	Brandon J. Ellis
JIMMY CAMPBELL	James Nathan Hopkins
WAYNE WRIGHT	Geoff Packard
JEAN ANN RYAN / PRODUCTION ASSISTANT	Mary Callanan
TOM	Max Clayton
BETSY	Andrea Dotto
MR. JACKSON	Ryan Kasprzak
ENTERTAINMENT DIRECTOR	Morgan Marcell
OLIVER	Drew McVety
AL / JAMES HAUPT	Kevyn Morrow
JO	Jessica Lea Patty
ANDRE BARUCH	Jonathan Shew
ROGER COHEN	Ryan VanDenBoom

CHARACTERS

DONNY NOVITSKI – Approximately twenty-four years old, ruggedly handsome with his Italian and Polish heritage. A piano (and accordion) prodigy, he is passionate about swing music and writing his own songs. While clearly shining with that elusive star quality, he carries the dark weight of wartime experiences. Baritone/Tenor, B-flat 2 to B-flat 4.

JULIA TROJAN – Approximately twenty-four years old, beautiful in a wholesome and effortless way. A gifted singer, but one without the drive to be a star. Her talents are personal to her and not showy, a means of expression and discovery. She is smart, honest, and no one's fool. Her star quality is born of her natural ability to simply tell the truth when singing; she is emotionally translucent on a stage. Soprano with strong belt, G3 to F-sharp 5.

MRS. JUNE ADAMS – Mid-forties to mid-fifties, she is Julia's mother and a woman of very modest means. She has a nervous anxiety most of the time and a desire to please that belies a personal history filled with disappointment and loss. Out of this energy comes her very quirky sense of comedy. But her grounded honesty is never far away when it comes to Julia's happiness. Alto, G3 to B4.

WAYNE WRIGHT – Late twenties to late thirties, he is a gifted jazz trombone player and a veteran Marine Lieutenant. Wayne manifests his war experiences in a severe case of obsessive compulsive disorder. He carries enormous tension in his body and mind and maintains an aloofness that hides his emotional turmoil. He is a man that can be very intimidating in his silence. High Baritone, C3 to B-flat 4.

JIMMY CAMPBELL – Late twenties to mid-thirties, he is a gifted jazz reed player, predominantly saxophone and clarinet. Jimmy is very bookish, thin, and well put together. He is wisely studying law, having just returned from the Navy. He has a careful and guarded personality but is fiercely loyal to Donny and the band. While the text never gives him away, Jimmy is privately gay and committed to fighting injustices in whatever ways he can. Baritone, C3 to G-sharp 4.

JOHNNY SIMPSON – Mid-twenties to late thirties, he is a drumming phenomenon. A returning Army Private, he suffers from severe back pain due to an injury requiring three surgeries. He is therefore reliant on pain medication, which affects his mental clarity. He also shows signs of traumatic head injury with memory loss. But mostly this all combines to give Johnny an almost childlike and gentle personality. He is by no means stupid – he has very honest insight – but he carries a charming simplicity that is in contrast to his sharp and impressive musical skills. High Baritone, B2 to G-sharp 4.

DAVY ZLATIC – Late twenties to early forties, he is a wiz on the upright bass. A recent Army veteran who served in the European theater and liberated Dachau, Davy is modeled heavily on Shakespeare's lovable Falstaff. A big man of big appetites, he drinks to no end and maintains a constant stream of silly jokes to entertain. He is an incredible talent and a loyal friend, playing the clown but in reality the protector. Baritone, B2 to F-sharp 4.

NICK RADEL – Late twenties to early forties, he is a genius trumpet player. A recent veteran of the Army who spent the last months of the European battles in a German prisoner-of-war camp, Nick is a man desperate for career and personal security. He is outrageously confident in his gifts as a musician and always on the lookout for those who would shortchange him of his deserved credit and compensation. Everything seems to be a personal affront to him and he has not yet been able to stop fighting for his life every day since returning to the home front. He prides himself on his ability to play exceptionally high notes on his trumpet and sometimes has a hard time being a team player. Baritone, B2 to F4.

JEAN ANN RYAN – Mid-thirties to late fifties, a glamorous local radio personality. Jean Ann prides herself on being the voice of several of WTAM Radio's most popular programs. She believes herself to be more worldly and sophisticated than she likely is, but her outsized persona is matched by a sentimental and dramatic heart. A voice that recalls early Judy Garland and Kate Smith, she is a warm alto.

OLIVER – Mid-forties to early sixties, a magnanimous owner of one of Cleveland's most popular nightclubs. The club that bears his name may not be the fanciest in town, but it is respected for its music scene. Oliver treats his guests like family and enjoys the spotlight whenever possible. Ensemble vocal track.

AL – Mid-forties to early sixties, an elegant and gracious owner of the most prestigious supper club in Cleveland, The Pavilion. He is suave and attentive to his guests but carries the confidence of the upper classes of Midwestern society. Ensemble vocal track.

JO – Late twenties to early fifties, a forthright owner of the hole-in-the-wall jazz club The Blue Wisp. Jo is a woman in a man's game and has incredible confidence. She's possibly pretty masculine herself and doesn't care who knows it. She's proud of her little club and loyal to her musicians and her decidedly blue-collar clientele. Ensemble vocal track.

ANDRE BARUCH – Mid-forties to mid-fifties, the real-life radio host and personality of several popular radio programs on NBC Radio in New York City. Andre is debonair and sincere with a classic radio voice that has the trained Mid-Atlantic accent of the time. Ensemble vocal track.

ROGER COHEN – Late twenties to early fifties, a corporate businessman in the much larger entertainment machine of the National Broadcasting Company. Roger is officious, efficient, and very good at his job. While he enjoys show business and is comfortable and confident in its rarified world, he has no patience for conflict. Ensemble vocal track.

JAMES HAUPT – Early thirties to early fifties, a successful director of radio programs at NBC Radio in New York City. He has the slickness of a New York show business professional with all the attendant charm and smarts. He always appears genuine and gracious when dealing with the "talent," but is all business behind the scenes. Ensemble vocal track.

PAULA – A woman of indiscriminate age, a no-nonsense New Yorker in the heart of the professional radio entertainment capital of the world. Ensemble vocal track.

BETSY – Late teens, an excitable bobby-soxer fan of the Donny Nova Band. She is all smiles and enthusiasm when meeting her favorite band. Her comic sense comes out of her blithe honesty and unabashed love of the music. Ensemble vocal track.

ENSEMBLE – Includes various **SERVICEMEN**, **CLUB PATRONS**, **SWING DANCERS**, **WAIT STAFF**, **RADIO STAFF**, **STAGEHANDS**, **JAZZ MUSICIANS**, **CLEVELANDERS**, and **NEW YORKERS**.

SETTING

Between late summer and December of 1945
in Cleveland, Ohio and New York City

ACT I

Scene One

(The time: August through December 1945.)

(The place: Cleveland, Ohio and New York City.)

(Bandstand *is intended to be played on as simple a set as possible, allowing for fluid transitions between sparsely suggested locations.)*

[MUSIC NO. 01 – PROLOGUE]

(In the darkness, a powerful rumbling and percussive explosions accelerate into a drum pattern. Slashes of light reveal two images. First, two soldiers huddled together as if in a trench as mortar shells explode around them. Second, a young woman, **JULIA TROJAN***, sitting in the tranquility of her home beside a radio, writing in her poetry journal. The two soldiers,* **DONNY NOVITSKI** *and* **MICHAEL TROJAN***, try to see above the trench at the enemy. Sensing* **DONNY***'s panic,* **MICHAEL** *steadies him by repeating what sounds like a refrain of reassurance.)*

MICHAEL. *(Calling and signaling to another foxhole.)* Hey, Rico! This is it.

(To **DONNY***.)* Novitski. Novitski! Hey, Nova!

THERE IS A TRAIN
We get some guys and go to New York.
THERE IS A TRAIN

IT LEAVES THE STATION
AT A QUARTER AFTER FIVE

Come on! The Cleveland Limited, go on –

DONNY.

AND IT'S DIRECT

MICHAEL. That's right.

FROM UNION TERMINAL
RIGHT THERE IN PUBLIC SQUARE

DONNY & MICHAEL.

A QUARTER AFTER FIVE

MICHAEL. That's right!

AND WHERE DOES IT ARRIVE?

(Calling and signaling again to foxholes on either side.)
Hey, Morris. We're gonna need cover! Rico, I need you,
brother.

*(To **DONNY**.)* Alright. Nova! Grenade on my go. Go!

DONNY. *(Yelling.)* Get out!

(There is a flash of light and an explosion.)

*(**JULIA** stands and moves away from the radio as the image of **DONNY** and **MICHAEL** in the foxhole vanishes. Several **SOLDIERS** begin to appear in their own time and space to take their place in a central formation. **DONNY** joins them. He is dressed in his United States Army uniform, a stuffed duffel bag over his shoulder.)*

*(An **OFFICER** appears in isolation and approaches **JULIA**, who now stands with her mother, **MRS. ADAMS**. The **OFFICER** hands **JULIA** a telegram. **JULIA** reads the telegram and collapses into her mother's arms. The officer salutes and moves away as **MRS. ADAMS** guides **JULIA** off into the darkness.)*

[MUSIC NO. 01A – JUST LIKE IT WAS BEFORE]

*(The **SOLDIERS** suddenly break from their formation, returning from the war, running into the arms of their girlfriends and family who appear throughout the space. The space becomes a chaotic swirl of motion, the images of America giddy with victory – ticker tape parades, dancing in the streets.)*

*(A piano appears and **DONNY** moves toward it. He sets down his duffel bag and removes his coat. We see now that **DONNY** is twenty-four years old, fit, and handsome in a unique, American melting pot kind of way. A radio appears opposite the piano and we are aware of **DONNY** in his small studio apartment in Cleveland, Ohio. He touches the piano like it's the only family he came home to. His sense of melancholy is in stark contrast to the victorious atmosphere just outside his door. In isolation, amid the celebration, local radio host **JEAN ANN RYAN** appears at a WTAM microphone. She is flanked by a trio of **STUDIO SINGERS**.)*

JEAN ANN. Cleveland's WTAM Radio with a special song to celebrate our victory.

*(The **STUDIO SINGERS** lean into the microphone and sing in close 1940s harmony.)*

JEAN ANN & STUDIO SINGERS.
THE BOYS ARE COMING HOME,
THE FLAGS ARE FLYING HIGH
AND MOM HAS BAKED HER SPECIAL APPLE PIE
YOU HUG YOUR GIRL
WHEN YOU WALK THROUGH THE DOOR
BEFORE YOU KNOW IT
IT'LL BE JUST LIKE IT WAS BEFORE
THE BAND IS TUNING UP
TO PLAY YOUR FAV'RITE SONG

JEAN ANN.

SO LIKE YOU USED TO
COME AND SING ALONG

AND THERE ARE ENDLESS
CAREFREE DAYS IN STORE

JEAN ANN.

BEFORE YOU KNOW IT

STUDIO SINGERS.

KAPOW!

JEAN ANN.

IT'LL BE

STUDIO SINGERS.

DOO DOOT DOO
DOO DOOT DOO
COME SING ALONG
AHH

JEAN ANN & STUDIO SINGERS.

JUST LIKE IT WAS,
IT'LL BE JUST LIKE IT WAS,
IT'LL BE JUST LIKE IT WAS BEFORE

DONNY.

FINALLY HOME
AND FINALLY SAFE
AND FINALLY FREE!

JEAN ANN & STUDIO SINGERS.

AHH

AHH

DONNY, JEAN ANN & STUDIO SINGERS.

SOON IT WILL BE
JUST LIKE IT WAS BEFORE

> (**JEAN ANN** *and the* **STUDIO SINGERS** *disappear as the scene shifts and the space is filled with* **SWING DANCING COUPLES** *of all ages.*)

[MUSIC NO. 01B – THE PAVILION]

> (**DONNY** *and his piano disappear as the space becomes the Pavilion nightclub.*)

SWING DANCING COUPLES.

IT'S LIKE THEY POPPED A CORK,
THE CLUBS ARE FULL AGAIN

SWING DANCING MEN.

WITH ALL THE GOOD TIME GIRLS

SWING DANCING WOMEN.
AND SERVICE MEN

SWING DANCING COUPLES.
SO GRAB YOUR SWEETHEART TIGHT
AND TAKE THE FLOOR
BEFORE YOU KNOW IT
IT'LL BE JUST LIKE IT WAS BEFORE

> (**DONNY** *re-enters, dressed for the evening.* **AL**, *the owner of the Pavilion, sees* **DONNY** *and crosses to him.*)

AL. Good lord, it's Donny Novitski. How long you been back, soldier?

DONNY. Couple days.

AL. How about my house band, huh?

DONNY. You need me up there on the keys.

AL. I'm all booked here. But something'll turn up. The cream always rises to the top, kid.

> (**AL** *motions to a* **WAITER** *and exits. The* **DANCING COUPLES** *take focus.*)

DONNY.
ALL THESE SWANKY CLUBS,

ENSEMBLE.
IT'S BEEN FAR TOO LONG

DONNY.
I OWNED THIS SCENE

ENSEMBLE.
IT'S GOOD TO HAVE YA BACK

DONNY.
I PLAYED EV'RY
ONE
AT SEVENTEEN

ENSEMBLE.
WANNA CUT A RUG WITH ME?

SWING DANCING MEN.
THE LIFE WE LEFT HAS BEEN HERE WAITING!

SWING DANCING WOMEN.
ISN'T THAT WORTH CELEBRATING?

(The scene shifts to a local VA office. The **SERVICEMEN** *seen dancing at The Pavilion disengage and take their places in the VA office as the other* **DANCERS** *disappear. The* **SERVICEMEN** *are filling out paperwork for GI Bill benefits. A female* **DESK CLERK** *appears.)*

[MUSIC NO. 01C – THE VA OFFICE]

DESK CLERK. *(Calls to the room.)* Private First Class Donald Novitski? Donald Novitski, please?

SERVICEMEN.

BEFORE YOU KNOW IT

*(***DONNY** *enters.)*

DONNY.

HERE

(The **DESK CLERK** *hands* **DONNY** *a clipboard of forms.)*

DESK CLERK. Fill these out please. Both sides on that one. Signature there, there, and there. Back to me when you're done.

DONNY. Yes, ma'am.

SERVICEMEN.

IT'LL BE JUST LIKE IT WAS BEFORE

*(***DONNY** *sits next to* **SERVICEMAN 1** *to fill out his forms.)*

SERVICEMAN 1. What division?

DONNY. Thirty-seventh.

SERVICEMAN 1. What was that, Solomon Islands?

DONNY. Yeah. And Bougainville.

SERVICEMAN 1. Shit. That must've been holy hell.

DONNY. Somethin' like that.

SERVICEMAN 1. When'd you get back?

DONNY. Couple weeks ago.

SERVICEMAN 1. Doing cash or college?

DONNY. I need the cash.

SERVICEMAN 1. Well find something quick, pal. I been to three funerals this month. Nobody's talkin' about it 'cause those guys came back fine a *while* ago.

DONNY. What happened?

SERVICEMAN 1. They wanted a way to make it stop. Find something quick.

DESK CLERK. *(Calling the next name on her list.)* Corporal Beiting. John Beiting.

> *(**DONNY** gets up and crosses to the **DESK CLERK** to hand in his forms. He moves to leave the VA hall. **SERVICEMEN** move forward as the scene begins to shift behind them. Two other **DESK CLERKS** appear.)*

SERVICEMEN.
   IT'LL BE JUST LIKE IT WAS BEFORE

DESK CLERK.
   SIGNATURE THERE, THERE, THERE

DESK CLERK 2.
   SIGNATURE THERE, THERE, THERE

DESK CLERK 3.
   SIGNATURE THERE, THERE, THERE

[MUSIC NO. 01D – DONNY'S ROOM]

> *(The **SERVICEMEN** exit as the scene gradually shifts. The piano in Donny's studio apartment appears. **DONNY** remains center as various people cross as if with the passage of time.)*

DONNY.
   I'D LIKE A GOOD NIGHT'S SLEEP

TALENT BOOKER. Our roster is pretty full. And our patrons come to hear the standards, not original tunes.

DONNY.
   IS THAT TOO MUCH TO ASK?

AL. A pal of mine needs an accordion player for a wedding. You still do that?

DONNY.

I NEED A SHOT OF WHISKY,
ALLS I GOT'S AN EMPTY FLASK

(It is the middle of the night. **DONNY** *goes to his radio and turns it on.* **JEAN ANN***'s voice is heard through the radio.)*

JEAN ANN.

BEFORE YOU KNOW IT,
IT'LL BE JUST LIKE IT WAS BEFORE

*(***DONNY** *stands as if in a daze, lost in memories. Out of the darkness around him appear disjointed images like unfocused daydreams: the two* **SOLDIERS** *in the foxhole from the opening image, another* **SOLDIER** *reaching for a grenade, yet another* **SOLDIER** *diving for cover. There are the sounds and lights of artillery explosions.)*

DONNY. *(Voice-over, as if in his head.)* Get out!

[MUSIC NO. 01E – JUST LIKE IT WAS BEFORE (FINALE)]

*(***DONNY** *recoils and reaches for the piano to steady himself. He begins to play maniacally a jazzy version of "Just Like It Was Before." The world around him swings into more of a celebration he can't connect to.)*

ENSEMBLE.

WE'RE ON A WINNING STREAK,
AND IT WILL STAY THAT WAY
WE'RE ON AN EVERLASTING HOLIDAY
AND ANY BAD NEWS YOU CAN JUST IGNORE
BEFORE YOU KNOW IT

(The scene shifts again as **DANCING COUPLES** *and various* **ENSEMBLE MEMBERS** *begin to appear out of the darkness, gathering upstage around a small stage to watch a singer in dim backlight.* **MR. JACKSON***, a smug jazz*

club owner, enters and crosses to **DONNY**. *The scene reveals another club, another audition.* **MR. JACKSON** *is counting a large roll of cash.* **DONNY** *is distracted by it – it's like waving a steak in front of a starving person.)*

DONNY. I'll take the slow nights.

ENSEMBLE.
   WE'RE ON A WINNING STREAK

MR. JACKSON. But see, we just got a new headliner.

ENSEMBLE.
   AND IT WILL STAY THAT WAY

MR. JACKSON. Just eighteen years old, baby face, the gals love him.

ENSEMBLE.
   WE'RE ON AN EVERLASTING HOLIDAY

DONNY. I'm sure I was playing circles around him when I was eighteen.

MR. JACKSON. Yeah, well, you're not eighteen now, are ya?

ENSEMBLE.
   AND ANY BAD NEWS YOU CAN JUST IGNORE

DONNY. *(Desperate humor.)* Some of us had a little service to take care of. Maybe you saw something in the papers.

ENSEMBLE.
   BEFORE YOU KNOW IT...

MR. JACKSON. Look, we're all thankful for your service, but I got nothin' for you here.

   (**MR. JACKSON** *stuffs the cash in his pocket, picks up a crate of liquor bottles, and begins to walk away.)*

DONNY.

Come on, I'm dyin' here. The whole town's giving me the same runaround. The only thing I live for is to play, and if I can't play, what's the use of me makin' it back?

ENSEMBLE.

AHH

AHH

MR. JACKSON.	ENSEMBLE.
That's a bit dramatic. You wanna try out for the community theater guild, they're down the block.	AHH

> (**DONNY** *begins to walk away, but then his rage gets the best of him and he violently smashes the crate out of* **MR. JACKSON***'s hands and onto the floor with the sound of shattering glass bottles. A* **BOUNCER** *appears behind* **DONNY** *and grabs him.* **DONNY** *struggles out of his grip and throws a punch at the* **BOUNCER.** **MR. JACKSON** *moves in to join the fight. The* **DANCING COUPLES** *and* **ENSEMBLE** *take more focus, their celebration becoming ever more overwhelming.* **DONNY** *remains in the center of it all, perpetuating the fight as a way to vent his rage even as he is beaten harder. His piano reappears out of the chaos.)*

ENSEMBLE.

	BAND.
IT'LL BE JUST LIKE IT WAS	WELCOME HOME
IT'LL BE JUST LIKE IT WAS	WELCOME HOME
IT'LL BE	

ENSEMBLE & BAND.

JUST LIKE IT WAS

DONNY.

	ENSEMBLE .
THAT'S WHAT THEY TELL ME	DOO BA DAP

ENSEMBLE & BAND.

WHY NOT BELIEVE IT?	DOO BA DA DAT DAT
THEY WANT ILLUSION	AHH
AND THEY ACHIEVE IT	
WE ALL RELIVE THE PAST	
AND NEVER WANT TO LEAVE IT	
THE WORLD IS ENDING	
AND WE'RE JUST PRETENDING	

ENSEMBLE & BAND.
FINALLY SAFE,
FINALLY FREE,
FINALLY HOME

ENSEMBLE.
IT'LL BE JUST LIKE IT WAS

*(***DONNY*** is tossed, beaten and bruised, as if out onto the street, but lands defeated on the bench of the piano in his sparsely furnished apartment. The tableau freezes.)*

*(***ANDRE BARUCH****, the dashing, mustachioed host/announcer of a radio program, appears at his NBC microphone. During his announcement, the ***DANCING COUPLES*** and ***ENSEMBLE*** fade into the darkness. ***DONNY*** leans against the piano as if listening to the radio.)*

[MUSIC NO. 01F – ANDRE BARUCH (UNDERSCORE)]

ANDRE BARUCH. This is Andre Baruch for The American Songbook of Popular Music, brought to you by Bayer Aspirin. NBC Radio and Metro-Goldwyn-Mayer are looking for the next great swing band to write their very own song in honor of our boys in uniform. Yes, it's "The American Songbook's Tribute to the Troops." A winning band from each state will compete in a nationwide broadcast, live from the Palace Theatre in New York on December sixteenth – to determine who will appear in a spectacular new motion picture musical, and be immortalized in Hollywood history.

[MUSIC NO. 02 – DONNY NOVITSKI]

*(***ANDRE BARUCH*** disappears into the darkness as ***DONNY*** at his piano takes full focus.)*

DONNY.
THAT'S ME
TO A TEE
HE MIGHT AS WELL HAVE SAID,

"HEY DONNY, COME AND GET YOUR PRIZE."
I COULD WRITE IT IN MY SLEEP
BUT THE TRICK IS THE DELIVERY
AND THE DIFF'RENCE THAT I HAVE
IS I WAS THERE
MADE IT THROUGH
AND NOW MY NUMBER ONE PRIORITY
IS TO PUT A BAND TOGETHER THAT DID TOO
EV'RY HORN AND CLARINET
WILL BE A MILITARY VET
AND BE PLAYING WITH AUTHORITY

DONNY NOVITSKI,
ACCORDION GENIUS
PLAYS WEDDINGS AT SEVEN YEARS OLD
THEN THE PIANO
LIKE FISH TAKE TO WATER,
BY NINE IT'S FATS WALLER DOWN COLD
TUNES OF MY OWN
START TO WORK THEMSELVES OUT,
I'M A TWELVE-YEAR-OLD IRVING BERLIN
ALL OF THAT PROMISE
AND NONE OF THE PAYOFF,
I'M STILL PLAYING WEDDINGS
I TAKE ON MY DAY OFF
FROM BUMMIN' AROUND DRINKIN' GIN

THEY SAY CREAM RISES
BUT WHAT IF NOBODY TASTED?
IF THAT CREAM RISES
THEN SPOILS, IT'S GONNA BE WASTED

BUT DONNY NOVITSKI
COULD BE FRANK SINATRA
IF SOMEONE WOULD GIVE HIM A BREAK
'FACT I'D BE BETTER
'CAUSE I PLAY PIANO
AND HE CAN'T READ MUSIC, THE FAKE
DONNY NOVITSKI
SPENT FOUR YEARS IN BATTLE
I CARRY THE SCARS WHEN I CROON

FRANKIE SINATRA
SKIPPED OUT ON THE ARMY
AND HALF THE TIME SINGS OUT OF TUNE
He's so flat!

THEY SAY CREAM RISES
BUT WHAT IF NOBODY KNEW IT?
IF THAT CREAM RISES
AND ROTS, THEN SOMEBODY BLEW IT

DONNY NOVITSKI
IS FINALLY LOOKING
AT ONE LITTLE CRACK IN THE DOOR
GET IT TO OPEN
AND RIGHT THERE BEHIND IT
IS EV'RYTHING I'M WORKING FOR
PICTURE DONNY NOVITSKI
THE POLISH ITALIAN,
CROONIN' HIS TUNES
AND SMOKIN' HIS STOGIES
GENUINE VET OF
AN ARMY BATTALION
THIN TAILORED SUITS
IF I CUT OUT PEROGIES
BOBBY-SOXERS SWOON AT MY CHARMS
BACKED UP BY MY BROTHERS IN ARMS!

DONNY NOVITSKI
KNOWS THIS IS A LIFELINE,
A ONCE-A-MILLENIUM SHOT
I'M GONNA TAKE IT,
TAKE AIM AT MY TARGET
AND HIT IT WITH ALL THAT I GOT
DONNY NOVITSKI
HAS STRONG AMMUNITION
PLENTY OF TALENT
AND BURNING AMBITION
WHOSE SONGS ARE AUTHENTIC AS WELL
FROM LIVING THROUGH FOUR YEARS OF HELL
DONNY NEEDS SOMETHING

TO BLOCK OUT THE MEM'RIES
AND BREAK THIS INSOMNIA SPELL

THEY SAY CREAM RISES
BUT WHAT IF NOBODY TASTED?
IF THAT CREAM RISES
THEN SPOILS, IT'S GONNA BE WASTED
SO MAKE IT ALL WORTH IT
AND GIVE IT A MEANING,
GOING FROM CLEVELAND
TO HOLLYWOOD SCREENING
DONNY NOVITSKI
IS GONNA WIN FIRST PRIZE
DONNY NOVITSKI
IS READY TO
RISE

(**DONNY** *exits as the scene shifts.*)

Scene Two

[MUSIC NO. 02A – INTO THE BLUE WISP (INSTRUMENTAL)]

(*A* **BARTENDER** *for the Blue Wisp Jazz Club crosses with a crate of glasses.* **JO**, *the female owner, wipes off a table and chair she's arranging, as the Blue Wisp Jazz Club appears around the piano. It is early evening and the club is preparing to open.* **JIMMY CAMPBELL** *enters, carrying a saxophone case and a music folder of piano charts. He is in his late twenties, possibly early thirties, small in stature with handsome but delicate – some might say feminine – features.* **JIMMY** *puts the folder on the piano and begins to unpack his sax.*)

JIMMY. (*To the* **WAITRESS**.) How's the house tonight?

JO. Good. Lining up outside already.

JIMMY. And of course Skip's running late. If he wasn't such a good piano player, I swear I'd –

(**DONNY** *enters from somewhere inside the club.*)

DONNY. Hiya! I'm looking for Jimmy Campbell.

JIMMY. We're not open yet.

DONNY. The back door is. Did you used to play with a cat went by the name of Rubber?

JIMMY. The drummer?

DONNY. That's the one.

JIMMY. Maybe a few gigs right out of high school –

(**DONNY** *eagerly sits at the piano.*)

DONNY. And you went into the Air Corp?

(**DONNY** *begins to play a few chords.*)

JIMMY. Navy. What is this? My pianist'll be here any minute –

DONNY. I was Army. Thirty-seventh Infantry. Rubber said you can really swing.

JIMMY. If you wait in line and pay like everyone else you'll find out –

DONNY. Show me.

[MUSIC NO. 02B – TELL ME TONIGHT]

(**DONNY** *plays an intro chord.*)

You know "Tell Me Tonight"?

JIMMY. What are you smoking?

DONNY. What, you don't know "Tell Me Tonight"?

> (**JIMMY** *takes up his sax and easily riffs the song's melody brilliantly.* **DONNY** *plays along for eight or so bars.*)

My name's Donny. I'm thinking of starting a band. All vets.

JIMMY. I'm getting a law degree, so my time is –

DONNY. We'll make it work. There's this contest on the radio –

JIMMY. The NBC thing.

DONNY. Bingo. They just announced the statewide competition's gonna be here in Cleveland. We got the hometown advantage. Whadda ya say?

JIMMY. I suppose you'd be the bandleader?

DONNY. Naturally.

JIMMY. Is Rubber on drums?

DONNY. He didn't make it back.

JIMMY. Aw, jeez.

[MUSIC NO. 03 – I KNOW A GUY]

DONNY. So you know any other guys? Who served, but young, good looking like us.

JIMMY. It's radio. What does it matter?

DONNY. If we win, we get to be in the movies. You know any?

JIMMY.
>I KNOW A GUY
>HE KICKS IT ON BASS
>HIS REGULAR GIG IS AT OLIVER'S PLACE
>HE'S BETTER THAN ANYONE
>WHEN HE'S NOT HIGH

DONNY. (*Spoken in rhythm.*) Jesus.

JIMMY. (*Spoken in rhythm.*) He's army too.

DONNY. (*Spoken in rhythm.*) I'll take my chances.

JIMMY.
>THEN YEP, I CAN TELL YOU
>THAT I KNOW A GUY

Meet me at the Rio Lounge tomorrow night.

DONNY. Wow! He plays at the Rio?!

JIMMY. No. He drinks there.

JO. We're ready to open, Jimmy.

JIMMY. Let 'em all in.

>(**DANCING COUPLES** *stream into the club and
>take to the floor as* **DONNY** *and* **JIMMY** *start to
>riff on the song. The scene shifts to the bar of
>The Rio Lounge.* **DAVY ZLATIC** *appears at the
>center of the bar, surrounded by a few buddies.*
>**DAVY** *is a stout guy, some might say a teddy
>bear, who carries the weight of all the beer he
>drinks. But he is nonetheless a riotous clown.
>He exudes life, albeit sometimes desperately
>and dangerously.*)

DAVY. Here's another one! A pirate walks into a bar with
his ship's steering wheel on the front of his pants. The
bartender says, "Captain, ya got a steering wheel stuck
to your crotch." The pirate says, "Aaargh, it's drivin' me
nuts!"

>(**JIMMY** *enters the lounge, leading* **DONNY**.)

DAVY. Jimmy!! You skinny son of a bitch. "What wind blew
you hither?"

JIMMY. This is Donny Novitski. Donny, meet Davy Zlatic. Donny here made it through Solomon Islands.

DAVY. "I'll tickle your catastrophe" – I liberated Dachau.

DONNY. Jeez.

DAVY. Jimmy told me about your band idea. I asked around about you.

(*To his buddies.*) So my cousin marries some Polack and it turns out this guy played accordion at her wedding when he was something like ten years old.

DONNY. You know the difference between an accordion and Hitler?

DAVY. Nope.

DONNY. One perpetrated years of oppression and humiliation on the Polish people. And the other's Hitler.

(**DAVY** *bursts into laughter.*)

DAVY. "I am not only witty in myself, but the cause that wit is in other men!"

DONNY. I have no idea what you're saying but I hope it means you're in.

JIMMY. It's Shakespeare. And yeah, he's in.

DONNY. Great. Now all we need are a couple of horns and a monster on drums.

DAVY.

I KNOW A GUY,
HIS TRUMPET IS HOT
A BARREL OF LAUGHS THOUGH,
THIS BASTARD IS NOT
BUT MAYBE WE'LL BREAK HIM
BETWEEN YOU AND I

DONNY. Let's do it.

DAVY.

THEN GET YOUR JOKES READY
'CAUSE I KNOW A GUY

(*The* **DANCING COUPLES** *take to the floor as the scene shifts.* **DAVY, DONNY,** *and* **JIMMY** *exit*

as the bar at The Rio Lounge disappears. The
DANCING COUPLES *recede into the darkness as*
NICK RADEL *appears with his trumpet in his*
music teaching studio. He is an intense and
impatient man. A young trumpet **STUDENT**
appears with him, obviously nervous.)

NICK. Take it again from bar four.

> *(The* **STUDENT** *plays a few bars of a jazz tune,*
> *missing several notes.)*

Stop.

> *(The* **STUDENT** *continues to play.)*

For the love of God, stop! What is that note right there?

STUDENT. B-flat.

NICK. How do you miss a B-flat? It's a B-flat trumpet!

STUDENT. I'm trying my best Mr. Radel.

NICK. I know. Heartbreaking, isn't it? I'll see you next week. And ask your father if he has the money to get your teeth fixed. Maybe that'll help.

> *(The* **STUDENT** *packs his case to exit as* **DAVY**
> *and* **DONNY** *enter the studio.)*

DAVY. Jeez, Nick, you tryin' for Teacher of the Year?

NICK. Screw you.

DAVY. This is the guy who thinks we belong in a band together.

NICK. Who else is on trumpet? I'm not playing second.

DONNY. Just you. We need a trombone though.

DAVY. And a drummer.

DONNY. Has to have served.

NICK.

> I KNOW A GUY
> A FORMER MARINE
> HE BLOWS LIKE A CHAMP
> AND HIS LICKS ARE OBSCENE
> A BUG UP HIS ASS

BUT I'D SAY WORTH A TRY
'CAUSE IF YOU WANT PERFECT,
THEN I KNOW A GUY

ENSEMBLE.

DOO, DOO, DOO, BA BA

(The scene begins to shift around them as **DONNY** *remains in solo isolation, realizing his plan is actually happening.)*

DONNY.

BOBBY-SOXERS SWOON	**ENSEMBLE.**
AT MY CHARMS	HE'S SO
	HE'S SO
	HE'S SO
BACKED UP BY MY	
BROTHERS	DOO DOOT DOO
IN ARMS	DOO DOOT DOO
	DOO DOOT DOO
	HE'S SO, HE'S SO
IS IT HAPPENING?	ONE OF A KIND
I THINK IT'S	
REALLY HAPPENING!	
I HEAR IT IN,	
"WE'RE READY TO OPEN"	READY READY READY
"LET 'EM ALL IN"	TO OPEN
"I AM NOT	LET 'EM IN THE PLACE
PLAYING SECOND!"	LET 'EM IN
"YEAH THAT MEANS	NOT PLAYING SECOND
HE'S IN"	LET 'EM IN

DONNY & ENSEMBLE.

FINALLY HOME

DONNY.

AND

DONNY & ENSEMBLE.

FINALLY SAFE
AND

DONNY.

FINALLY FREE...

ENSEMBLE. *(Variously.)*
>FINALLY FREE
>FINALLY FREE

>>(**WAYNE WRIGHT** *appears in his own time and space holding his trombone. He is an imposing and militaristic man, tightly wound and oddly ritualistic.* **DONNY** *approaches* **WAYNE,** *and they are in mid-conversation as a* **STAGE MANAGER** *walks past them.)*

STAGE MANAGER.	**ENSEMBLE.**
Five minutes to places, everyone.	OOO, OOO
Five minutes.	

ENSEMBLE MEN.
>TIME TO OPEN UP

ENSEMBLE WOMEN.
>GOTTA OPEN UP THE DOORS

ENSEMBLE MEN.
>OPEN UP

ENSEMBLE.
>WE GOT A SHOW AT EIGHT

WAYNE.
>I KNOW A GUY
>HE'S KIND OF A MESS
>HE MADE IT BACK HOME IN ONE PIECE
>MORE OR LESS
>A GENIUS ON DRUMS,
>THOUGH ON BRAIN MATTER SHY

WAYNE.	**ENSEMBLE.**
BUT, MAN, YOU WANT RHYTHM	OOO
THEN I KNOW A GUY	

DONNY.	**JIMMY & ENSEMBLE.**	**ENSEMBLE.**
IT'S HAPPENING	HE KICKS IT ON BASS	HE'S SO
		OOO

DAVY & ENSEMBLE.		JIMMY & ENSEMBLE.	
HIS TRUMPET IS HOT		HIS REGULAR GIG	

DONNY.	NICK & ENSEMBLE.	ENSEMBLE.
IT'S ALL	A FORMER MARINE	HE'S SO

DONNY.	JIMMY & ENS.	DAVY & ENS.	WAYNE & ENS.	ENS.
HAPPENING	IS AT OLIVER'S	A BARREL OF LAUGHS THOUGH,	HE'S KIND OF A MESS	OOO

JIMMY & ENSEMBLE.	NICK & ENSEMBLE.
PLACE	HE BLOWS LIKE A CHAMP

DAVY & ENS.	NICK & ENS.	WAYNE & ENS.	ENS.
THIS BASTARD IS NOT	AND HIS LICKS ARE OBSCENE	A GENIUS ON DRUMS	HE'S SO

DONNY.	WAYNE & ENS.	ENSEMBLE.
IT'S ALL HAPPENING	THOUGH ON BRAIN MATTER SHY	ONE OF A KIND

ENSEMBLE.
IF YOU WANT ONE OF A KIND,
THEN YEP I CAN TELL YA
THAT I KNOW A GUY

(*The scene shifts instantly to reveal the piano in the Blue Wisp Jazz Club, now flanked by* **JOHNNY SIMPSON** *playing a drum set,* **DAVY** *playing his upright bass, and* **JIMMY** *playing his sax.* **DONNY** *crosses in and takes his seat at the piano just as* **NICK**, *trumpet in hand, positions himself next to* **JIMMY**. **WAYNE** *crosses in from the other side to join them all with his trombone. The band is complete. They are in full swing before a small group of* **CLUBGOERS**.)

[MUSIC NO. 03A - AIN'T WE PROUD]

DONNY.

> I KNOW A GUY
> YOU'D NEVER GUESS WOULD BE A HERO,
> JUST SOME MELLOW
> AV'RAGE FELLOW
> TO LOOK AT YOU MIGHT SAY,
> "WELL, HE'D AMOUNT TO ZERO,"
> BUT IN COMBAT,
> THERE'S YOUR TOP CAT
> WHEN THE CHIPS WERE DOWN
> HE EARNED UNCLE SAM RENOWN
> NOW HE'S JUST RETURNED TO OUR HOME TOWN
> AND AFTER SUCH A VICT'RY
> YOU'LL FORGIVE ME
> BRAGGIN' A BIT OUT LOUD
> THE BOYS ARE BACK
> AND AIN'T WE PROUD!

> (**JIMMY, WAYNE,** and **NICK** play solos.)

DONNY.

> AND AFTER SUCH A VICT'RY,
> FIND US GLADLY
> GREETING THE CHEERING CROWD
> THE BOYS ARE BACK!

JIMMY, JOHNNY, DAVY, NICK & WAYNE.

> THE BOYS ARE BACK!

DONNY.

> THE BOYS ARE BACK!

JIMMY, JOHNNY, DAVY, NICK, WAYNE & ENSEMBLE.

> THE BOYS ARE BACK!

DONNY.

> YOU KNOW THE BOYS ARE BACK!
> AND AIN'T WE
> ROARIN' BACK AND AIN'T WE
> BACK ON TRACK AND AIN'T WE PROUD!

> (The **CLUBGOERS** applaud. **DONNY** gets up
> from the piano as **JO** exits and the **CLUBGOERS**
> begin to disperse.)

[MUSIC NO. 03B – AIN'T WE PROUD (PLAYOFF)]

ENSEMBLE.

> THE BOYS ARE BACK
> THE BOYS ARE BACK
> THE BOYS ARE BACK
> THE BOYS ARE BACK
> OH AH!

> (**JIMMY, DAVY, WAYNE, JOHNNY,** *and* **NICK** *begin packing up their instruments and music.*)

JOHNNY. I'm so glad I decided to play with you guys.

DONNY. Best decision of your life.

JOHNNY. No, that was holdin' onto the steering wheel while my jeep was flippin' three times. Three times, I'm tellin' ya.

DONNY. Three times, huh?

JOHNNY. Yeah, after the shell hit, three flips and three operations on my back. How 'bout that?

DONNY. That's somethin', Johnny.

JOHNNY. That reminds me – time to take my pain pill. Always *after* the gig 'cause they slow me down.

> (**JOHNNY** *takes a pill case from his pocket to take his pill.*)

DAVY. How much slower do you get? What do they put you in *reverse*?

> (*To* **DONNY.**) You write a catchy tune, Novitski.

NICK. (*Skeptically.*) Catchy enough to win a contest?

DONNY. (*Annoyed.*) I got more where that came from. And hotshot, next time you play a solo, get down off the ceiling once in a while. It's all one color, it's selfish.

NICK. I don't know how to break this to you – it's a "SOLO"! It's selfish by DEFINITION!

DONNY. It's outta line.

NICK. I can play with Dwight Anson – he's doin' the contest.

DONNY. *(Pointedly.)* Dwight Anson? You survive a POW camp to play with a hack like that?

NICK. Whadda you got that's better?

DONNY. *(Even more annoyed.)* The local broadcast is in three weeks. I wanna try out a few tunes and see what flies, and Jo agreed to let us play a set here Sunday night.

WAYNE. No. I have dinner with the family every Sunday.

DONNY. It'll be after dinner.

WAYNE. I don't go out late on a Sunday.

DAVY. So make it another night.

DONNY. *(Losing his patience.)* No! We're booked here for a set Sunday at nine. That's the deal.

WAYNE. In the future I need more notice. I need a schedule. I got a wife and kids and three other standing gigs.

NICK. How much is it gonna pay?

DONNY. When we win the contest –

WAYNE. Tonight was your only freebie, Private. Every gig I play is food and shoes for my kids.

DONNY. Alright, I'll make sure we get somethin'.

NICK. *(Demanding.)* Standard rate.

DONNY. Fine. Sunday. I'll have all the charts.

WAYNE. Sunday.

> *(**WAYNE** exits.)*

JOHNNY. *(Beat.)* So, what day of the week is Sunday?

DONNY. It's...*Sunday.*

JOHNNY. Yeah, that's fine, I'm not doin' anything. Anybody need a lift?

DAVY. Swing by the Rio?

JOHNNY. Sure.

DAVY. *(To **JOHNNY**.)* Hey kid, try this one. So a giraffe walks into a bar and says, "The highballs are on me!"

JOHNNY. I don't get it.

DAVY. Well you see, giraffes are really tall, so...

(**JOHNNY**, **DAVY**, *and* **NICK** *exit.*)

JIMMY. If you're going to be a bandleader you better learn how to talk to people.

DONNY. So now you're gonna pile on too?

JIMMY. I was on the Reid – the ship explodes and I'm in the water with my dead friends.

I play to forget that shit, not re-live it.

DONNY. So you're saying my band's a shipwreck?

(**JIMMY** *starts to pack and leave.*)

JIMMY. Just forget it. My class load's too heavy this semester. Find another sax player.

DONNY. *(Relenting.)* Wait, just wait. Rubber said you were good enough to go all the way to New York with us someday. You gonna throw that away?

JIMMY. That's kind but I barely remember the guy.

DONNY. He was my best buddy in the thirty-seventh. He made me promise to look in on his wife if anything happened to him. So...

JIMMY. So?

DONNY. So I'm an asshole 'cause I've been walking past her door and I can't make myself knock. She'll wanna know how it happened.

JIMMY. How bad was it?

DONNY. *(With difficulty.)* Bad.

(*Beat.*)

Friendly fire.

JIMMY. Don't tell her. Make sure she's okay. You owe him that. But here's some free legal advice: don't go to trial unless you're prepared to lose.

(*Reassuring.*) I'll see you Sunday.

[MUSIC NO. 03C – JULIA'S FRONT DOOR]

(*The scene shifts as* **DONNY** *begins to exit. Radio host* **JEAN ANN RYAN** *appears at a WTAM-NBC microphone.*)

JEAN ANN. Looking ahead to the end of the month, we're happy to announce our Tribute to the Troops contest will be broadcast from the beautiful Ohio Theatre. It'll be a special audience to be a part of as your applause will factor into our judges' decision.

> (**JEAN ANN** *and her microphone disappear into the darkness.*)

Scene Three

(Night becomes late afternoon the following day as the front door to the home of **JULIA ADAMS TROJAN** *appears.* **DONNY** *enters and approaches the door. He stands before it for a moment, gathering the courage to ring the doorbell. He rings, and with no immediate response, loses his nerve and begins to walk away.* **JULIA** *opens the door. She is in her early twenties and very pretty in an unusual way. She has a smart, bookish air about her, but her eyes are sad and regard the world cautiously. Her gestures are inhibited and protected. There is a resignation to her courtesy. She is wearing a kitchen apron and her hair is a bit untidy. She is also spattered with flour.)*

JULIA. *(Impatient.)* Yes?

    *(**DONNY** stares at her as if frozen.)*

    (Beat.)

Well, whatever you're selling, you gotta work on your sales pitch.

DONNY. You're Julia.

JULIA. Do I know you?

DONNY. I'm Donny Novitski.

MRS. ADAMS. *(From within.)* Who is it?

JULIA. *(Calling back, unsettled.)* It's a friend of Michael's, Ma.

DONNY. I would've called first, but I didn't have the number.

JULIA. I didn't mean to be rude. I was baking a cake for church, and I just –

DONNY. I don't want to bother you.

JULIA. No bother. He mentioned you a lot in his letters. How'd you find me?

DONNY. Michael gave me the address.

JULIA. *(Beat.)* And you're supposed to check in on me.

DONNY. I'm just awfully sorry –

> *(**DONNY** freezes, and there is a tense moment where **JULIA** wonders if he is about to become overwhelmed emotionally.)*

JULIA. *(At a loss.)* Well, I'm getting along.

DONNY. Good to hear.

JULIA. Come in. Please.

DONNY. Well, your mother –

JULIA. She'll want to meet you –

DONNY. Maybe another time. I should go.

JULIA. Nonsense. Come in.

DONNY. I'm supposed to meet some friends –

JULIA. You don't stop here on your way to meet friends. *(Long beat.)* You could come for dinner sometime.

DONNY. I don't want to impose.

JULIA. How about Thursday. Say five-thirty?

DONNY. Sure. If you're sure.

JULIA. See you then.

[MUSIC NO. 03D – PROUD RIFF]

> *(The scene shifts as **DONNY** exits and **JULIA** closes the door behind her.)*

Scene Four

*(On the home front, **WAYNE** is seen obsessively cleaning a gun. His anxiety and compulsiveness are magnified in a tap-danced vision of other men having difficulty reintegrating into the community. **WAYNE'S WIFE** enters just as he finishes.)*

WAYNE'S WIFE. Sorry I'm late, Honey. How was your day?

ENSEMBLE. WAYNE!

WAYNE!

HAH! HAH! HAH! HAH! HAH!

AH AH AH AH AH AH AH

WAYNE. Fine.

WAYNE'S WIFE. Did you help Grady with his homework?

WAYNE. Didn't have time.

*(**WAYNE'S WIFE** exits as **WAYNE** fades into darkness.)*

[MUSIC NO. 03E - MRS. ADAMS (UNDERSCORE)]

*(The scene shifts to reveal the inside of Julia's home. It is the morning of Donny's visit. To one side is a modest dining table and chairs. There is also a piano in the room, near the door opposite the dining table. **MRS. ADAMS** enters the room from what is presumably the kitchen. She is well into middle age and has a grounded but somehow sad spirit that she attempts at all times to hide with manufactured cheer.)*

MRS. ADAMS. *(Calling off.)* We have a few bottles of Coca-Cola or he can have milk. Do you know what he likes to drink? Julia? Do you know what he drinks?

*(**JULIA** enters.)*

JULIA. I don't know him at all, Ma. I'm late for work.

MRS. ADAMS. *(The sadness creeping through.)* Was he with Michael when he died?

JULIA. He didn't say.

MRS. ADAMS. Then *don't* ask him. He'll tell you if he wants to. Remember your uncle never spoke a word about the first war after *he* got back. Not for the rest of his life.

JULIA. *(Sarcastically.)* So I don't ask questions, he doesn't talk, and we just sit across the table in silence.

MRS. ADAMS. Next to baseball, it's the national pastime.

JULIA. I just want to know what happened.

MRS. ADAMS. And what do you think that will get you?

JULIA. Sleeping through the night. Closing a chapter. Maybe just getting out of this door.

MRS. ADAMS. I didn't make you late. This time.

[MUSIC NO. 04 – WHO I WAS]

JULIA.
YOU KNOW WHAT I WANT EVEN MORE?
IS TO BE JUST WHO I WAS BEFORE

MRS. ADAMS. Pick up some ketchup on your way home.

> (**JULIA** *goes through the door as* **MRS. ADAMS** *fades into darkness. The scene suggests* **JULIA** *moving through her day.)*

JULIA.
SELF-ASSURED,
FUTURE ALL SECURED
THAT WAS JULIA.
QUICK TO TRUST,
SAW THE WORLD AS JUST
THAT WAS JULIA.
FULL OF PROMISE AND FULL OF POISE
HARDLY ANY OF WHICH THIS
SHOP GIRL NOW EMPLOYS
BUT I MUDDLE THROUGH...
EASY SMILE,
AVID CINEPHILE
THAT WAS JULIA

THAT WAS JULIA
BEFORE BEING BRANDED A GOLD STAR WIFE
A DISTINCTION THAT'S REDEFINING
MY WHOLE LIFE
WELL, IT FEELS LIKE IT DOES
I FEEL GUILTY BECAUSE
THERE ARE DAYS WHEN I JUST WANT TO BE WHO I WAS

> *(The scene shifts around **JULIA**, returning her to her home.)*

Ma,

I'M NOT SAYING I'D TRADE
THE LIFE THAT I HAD
WITH HIM FOR A MINUTE
THAT WAS ONCE IN A LIFETIME LOVE
AND I KNOW I WAS LUCKY TO WIN IT
AND I'M TOLD TO BE PROUD
ALL THE NEWS REELS AND MAGAZINES
PRACTIC'LY SHOUT IT
BUT I'M NEVER ALLOWED
TO ADMIT THERE IS NOTHING
REMOTELY HEROIC ABOUT IT

> *(She stands next to **MRS. ADAMS** at the table.)*

AND YOU KNOW I WOULD NEVER BE ABLE
TO SAY THAT AWAY FROM THIS
DINING ROOM TABLE...
NOT A DOUBT
HOW HER LIFE PLAYS OUT
THAT WAS JULIA.
ALL THE DETAILS OF WHO I AM
MADE IRRELEVANT WITH ONE
SINGLE TELEGRAM
THAT'S WHAT WIDOWHOOD DOES
I RESENT IT BECAUSE
THERE ARE DAYS WHEN I JUST WANT TO BE
MOMENTARILY FREE
AND HAPPILY
WHO I WAS

(The doorbell rings.)

I'll get it.

*(**JULIA** exits toward the front door. **MRS. ADAMS** nervously adjusts the place settings.)*

MRS. ADAMS. People just don't arrive fashionably late anymore.

*(**JULIA** re-enters with **DONNY**. **DONNY** carries a photo album under his arm.)*

DONNY. Hiya. Boy, you look...very nice.

JULIA. Thanks. Come in. Ma, this is Donny Novitski.

DONNY. How do you do.

MRS. ADAMS. June Adams. Pleasure to meet you.

DONNY. *(Seeing the piano.)* Which one of you plays?

MRS. ADAMS. I used to, back in high school. Eighteen-seventy-six.

JULIA. You want to try it out?

DONNY. Maybe later.

MRS. ADAMS. Oh, I hope so. Have a seat at the table. I have to get busy in the kitchen but I have some deviled eggs you can have as a fancy appetizer. I'll have those out in a jiffy.

*(**MRS. ADAMS** exits. **DONNY** and **JULIA** sit at the table.)*

DONNY. Your mom's nice.

JULIA. She works hard at it.

DONNY. And your dad?

JULIA. Oh. He's traveling. For work. A salesman.

DONNY. What's he sell?

JULIA. Oh. Uh...Frigidaires. Of all things.

DONNY. Must be hard to lug around.

*(An awkward beat, as **JULIA** is uncertain if he's attempting a joke.)*

Michael talked about you working at Halle Brothers department store.

JULIA. The cosmetics counter.

DONNY. And you sing.

JULIA. I confine my singing to solos in church these days.

DONNY. I'd like to hear you.

JULIA. Well, unless you find yourself at Our Lady of Mercy this Sunday that's pretty unlikely.

> (**MRS. ADAMS** *enters with a plate of deviled eggs. She sets them on the table.*)

Wow... Mom?

MRS. ADAMS. The top of the paprika shaker fell off. Like they say, you can't put the genie back in the bottle. I am so sorry.

> (**MRS. ADAMS** *exits hurriedly.*)

JULIA. How embarrassing. Your mom's probably a gourmet cook.

DONNY. My mom passed when I was thirteen.

JULIA. Oh, I'm sorry.

DONNY. I haven't had a good home-cooked meal in I don't know how long, so I'm grateful for this. *(Placing the photo album on the table.)* Anyway, I brought these photos of Michael from when we were over there -

JULIA. Oh, let's see.

DONNY. Maybe we should wait till after dinner.

JULIA. Let's look now. It's fine.

[MUSIC NO. 04A – THE PHOTO ALBUM]

> (**DONNY** *shifts so they can both look at the photo album.* **JULIA** *takes a moment and then opens the cover.*)

DONNY. That was in boot camp when we met. *(Pointing.)* That picture's in Fiji, right after we landed. I had a tan about ten minutes off the boat 'cause I'm half Italian but he was full Polish, so...boiled lobster.

JULIA. *(Becoming very emotional.)* It happened every summer.

DONNY. Oh, here he is at –

>   (**DONNY** *notices* **JULIA** *is overwhelmed.*)

JULIA. I'm sorry –

DONNY. Why don't I just leave these with you. You can go through them later.

JULIA. That's probably a good idea.

DONNY. Yeah.

JULIA. *(Trying to lighten the mood.)* I see you wrote "Michael" on these. Is that what you called him?

DONNY. *(A bit embarrassed.)* Well, he did have a nickname –

JULIA. Rubber?

DONNY. Yeah, that's the one.

JULIA. He had it since high school. And I got really good at the jokes.

DONNY. Guess that's what you get with a last name like Trojan.

>   (*They enjoy a laugh.* **MRS. ADAMS** *enters.*)

MRS. ADAMS. Alrighty then, dinner's almost ready. Julia? Oh, you didn't touch the eggs.

JULIA. We'll have them with dinner.

>   (**MRS. ADAMS** *exits as* **JULIA** *rises.*)

Were you there?

DONNY. Where?

JULIA. Bougainville Island. When he died.

DONNY. *(Beat.)* Yeah.

JULIA. *(Beat.)* I hate deviled eggs. Be sure to tell my mom you like the roast. Even if you don't. It's her specialty.

>   (**JULIA** *exits for the kitchen. The scene shifts as Julia's home disappears into the darkness.*)

Scene Five

(**JOHNNY** *appears out of the darkness, flanked by the images of two fallen* **SERVICEMEN** *who seem to shadow his every move.* **JIMMY** *appears out of the darkness, weighed down by his own visible manifestation of a fallen comrade. He begins playing a sentimental solo melody on his sax. Gradually,* **NICK** *is revealed and joins in harmony on his trumpet, then* **WAYNE** *on trombone, then* **DAVY** *on his upright bass, and* **JOHNNY** *on his drums. As they play, the visible memories that each of them carry with them of the men they left behind in battle begin to leave them and vanish. Various* **ENSEMBLE** *members appear out of the darkness. They are gathering for church, but we see various vignettes of their daily lives as they prepare to go to mass: finishing touches on outfits, a last-minute bite of breakfast, a final glance at the funnies in the Sunday paper, even evidence of unhappy relationships. The* **ENSEMBLE** *begins to sing in perfect counterpoint to Donny's* **BAND** *which recedes further into the darkness as the church organ takes over.*)

[MUSIC NO. 05 – COUNTERPOINT / PIE JESU]

(**JULIA** *appears as if at the front of her church. By the end of Julia's song, the* **BAND** *at Donny's home has disappeared and we are at the altar of Our Lady of Mercy Church.*)

JULIA.
　　PIE JESU,
　　PIE JESU
　　QUI TOLLIS PECCATA MUNDI
　　PIE JESU,

PIE JESU
DONA EIS,
DONA EIS,
DONA EIS REQUIEM

ENSEMBLE.
AMEN

(The service has ended, and **JULIA** *begins to cross away from the front altar. In the shadows of the perimeter of the space,* **MEMBERS OF THE CONGREGATION** *pass by, greeting one another quietly and making their way out.* **MRS. ADAMS** *crosses to* **JULIA.** **DONNY** *appears from the shadows and approaches* **JULIA.***)*

DONNY You didn't tell me you got to do the big finale.

JULIA. *(Surprised.)* What are you doing here?

MRS. ADAMS. Well, he's here now. The choir could use a tenor under sixty.

JULIA. Ma!

DONNY. Your daughter's voice is beautiful.

JULIA. Thanks.

DONNY. *(To* **JULIA.***)* It's really high.

MRS. ADAMS. Can't keep a single wine glass in the house.

(She mimes glasses shattering.)

JULIA. Ma!

MRS. ADAMS. I'll see you outside.

*(**MRS. ADAMS** exits.)*

DONNY. Do you sing swing?

JULIA. I used to.

DONNY. I put this band together and we're playing a set tonight at the Blue Wisp and I was wondering if you'd come by to hear us.

JULIA. Tonight? Oh, I have work early tomorrow.

DONNY. It's just one set. Nine o'clock, and you'll be home by ten, I promise. Whadda ya say?

[MUSIC NO. 06 – JUST LIKE IT WAS (REPRISE)]

JULIA. The Blue Wisp?

DONNY. On Superior, and West Third.

JULIA. Nine o'clock?

DONNY. Just a half-hour set.

JULIA. Alright.

> (**JULIA** *exits as the scene begins to shift.*)

Scene Six

(The Blue Wisp Jazz Club appears, as **DANCING COUPLES** *take to the floor and mingle at their various tables.* **JULIA** *and* **MRS. ADAMS** *appear in isolation.* **MRS. ADAMS** *is fussing over* **JULIA**'s *attire.)*

ENSEMBLE.
BEFORE YOU KNOW IT
IT'LL BE JUST LIKE IT WAS BEFORE

MRS. ADAMS.
I THINK YOUR DRESS
LOOKS GREAT
AS I AM SURE HE'LL SAY
I KNOW IT'S NOT A DATE
SO DON'T YOU LOOK AT ME
THAT WAY
YOU JUST DESERVE
A BREAK
FROM STAYING HOME

WITH ME ALL DAY   **ENSEMBLE.**
I GOT THE RADIO   OOO
AND BOOKS TO READ
I'LL BE OKAY   BA DAP
I GOT A HUNDRED HANDS OF   OOO
SOLITAIRE
THAT I CAN PLAY   BAP BA DAP
AND IF YOU'RE
STILL OUT LATE   OOO
I'LL TEACH MYSELF
TO KNIT CROCHET

ENSEMBLE.
IT'S TIME FOR
THE PARTY TO START

MRS. ADAMS.
BEFORE YOU KNOW IT,

ENSEMBLE.
> BA DA BAP BAP BAP

MRS. ADAMS & ENSEMBLE.
> IT'LL BE JUST LIKE IT WAS BEFORE

> (**DAVY, JOHNNY, JIMMY, NICK,** *and* **WAYNE** *appear on the small center stage playing in full swing.* **DONNY** *crosses in and takes his place at the piano as* **JULIA** *enters and takes a seat at one of the tables.* **DONNY** *and the* **BAND** *finish a riff.* **DAVY** *and* **JOHNNY** *continue vamping the rhythm as* **DONNY** *talks to the crowd.)*

DONNY. Before we go, folks, there's a young gal here tonight, with a spectacular set of pipes and I'd love to have her sing something.

JULIA. *(Horrified.)* Donny, no.

WAYNE. What're you doing? You didn't say anything about this. What are we supposed to play?

DONNY. How about a standard, something everyone knows – that's why they're called standards, right Wayne?

JULIA. Donny...

DONNY. Give her a hand, folks. Julia Trojan. Come on up.

> (*The* **DANCING COUPLES** *applaud their approval and* **JULIA** *reluctantly takes the stage.)*

How about "First Steps"? You can do that, right?

JULIA. I guess I can try it.

WAYNE. What key?

DONNY. Put it in C, guys.

JOHNNY. Wait, I gotta transpose...

> (**JOHNNY** *hits his snare two times quickly.)*

DONNY. *(Rolling his eyes and counting the band in.)* Two, three, and...

[MUSIC NO. 07 – FIRST STEPS FIRST]

       (**DONNY** *starts the intro and the band picks*
       it up.)

JULIA.

    PARDON MY BRASHNESS DEAR,
    SEEING YOU STANDING HERE,
    DANCING'S MORE CUSTOMARY
    FOR A
    SOIRÉE
    ISN'T THE BAND SUBLIME?
    AND AS IT HAPPENS I'M
    JUST IN THE MOOD TO DO A
    TWO-STEP
    DO STEP
    OUT ON THE FLOOR WITH ME
    I'M NEW HERE TOO YOU SEE
    MIGHT YOU BE CHARMINGLY COERCED?
    NO NEED TO BE SO SHY
    TAKE REASSURANCE I
    KNOW HOW TO GUIDE YOU
    THROUGH THE WORST STEPS;
    FIRST STEPS FIRST

       (**JULIA** *suddenly can't remember the lyrics to*
       the bridge.)

I don't remember the bridge.

WAYNE. She doesn't remember the bridge.

DONNY. *(Trying to help her.)*
    WHY BE ALL ALONE –

       (**JULIA** *begins to walk away from the*
       microphone, terribly embarrassed.)

JULIA. I'm sorry.

DONNY. No wait. *(Stopping the **BAND**.)* It's my fault. The
tempo's all wrong, isn't it?

JULIA. I don't know –

DONNY. Yeah. Kick it up, Davy.

DAVY. Thank God.

(**DAVY** *suddenly kicks up the tempo with a walking bass line, and the rest of the* **BAND** *follows.*)

DONNY. (*To* **JULIA**, *spoken in rhythm.*) From the bridge. "Why be all alone…" You got it.

JULIA.

WHY BE ALL ALONE WHEN MUSIC CALLS?

DONNY. Now we're cookin'.

JULIA.

I HAVE NOTHING MORE OR LESS TO PROVE

DONNY. She's terrific folks!

JULIA.

BUT UNLESS WE WANT A PARTY
FULL OF FLOWERS ON THE WALLS,

JULIA & DONNY.

SOMEONE HAS TO MAKE THE VERY FIRST MOVE

JULIA.	**DONNY**.
STARTING	STARTING
IS DAUNTING, TRUE	
TRUSTING	TRUSTING
IN SOMETHING NEW	
FEARFUL YOUR LUCK	FEARFUL
WILL BE REVERSED	YOUR LUCK
BUT,	WILL BE REVERSED

JULIA & DONNY.

I HAVE A FEELIN' I'D
STEADY YOU IF YOU TRIED
SOON YOU'LL BE DANCIN'
THROUGH REHEARSED STEPS
FIRST STEPS FIRST

DONNY.

BAH BA DO 'N

JULIA & DONNY.

DAH DA
FIRST STEPS FIRST
FIRST STEPS FIRST!

(The **CLUB** *applauds excitedly as* **JO** *takes the mic.)*

JO. Wasn't she great?

[MUSIC NO. 07A – FIRST STEPS (PLAYOFF)]

*(***JULIA** *is flushed with a mixture of elation and embarrassed awkwardness.* **DONNY**, **JULIA***, and the* **BAND** *begin to leave the stage.)*

JULIA. *(Strongly.)* I can't believe you put me on the spot like that.

DONNY. Admit it, you're glad I got you up there.

JULIA. That's not an apology.

DONNY. *(Cutting her off.)* C'mon fellas.

*(***DONNY** *leads* **JULIA**, **JIMMY**, **DAVY**, **JOHNNY***, and* **NICK** *to a table.* **WAYNE** *remains behind, packing his trombone.)*

You can officially meet Julia.

(As **DONNY** *makes introductions,* **JULIA** *shakes their hands.)*

This is Davy Zlatic.

JULIA. *(Softening.)* How do you do.

DAVY. Can we get you a drink?

JULIA. Oh, I hardly ever drink.

DAVY. Wanna trade livers?

DONNY. And Jimmy Campbell.

JIMMY. So glad you came.

DONNY. And this is Johnny Simpson and Nick Radel.

NICK. Great chops, Miss. You should really sing pro.

JULIA. Oh, best I could hope for is to teach the kids choir at church.

NICK. Don't teach.

*(***WAYNE** *has finished packing and begins to approach the table.)*

DAVY. *(Conspiratorially to* **JULIA***.)* And here comes Lieutenant Wayne Wright. Now watch, he won't shake your hand 'cause he'd have to wash his own ten times after.

> (**WAYNE** *subtly avoids shaking* **JULIA***'s hand.*)

WAYNE. Ma'am. Sorry to bow out. Heading home. Goodnight, everyone.

> (**WAYNE** *starts to exit.*)

JULIA. *(Calling after him.)* Family?

WAYNE. *(Caught off guard.)* Yes, ma'am.

JULIA. Kids?

WAYNE. Jane and Grady.

JULIA. Well, they have a very talented father. Nice to meet you.

> (**WAYNE** *nods, unable to express his gratitude, and exits.*)

JOHNNY. *(To* **JULIA***.)* What's your last name again?

JULIA. Trojan. Go ahead, fill in your own joke.

JOHNNY. I only asked 'cause I have trouble remembering things. A shell hit my jeep and it flipped three times – three times, I'm tellin' ya.

JULIA. My goodness.

JOHNNY. I remember whole songs just listening once, but other stuff, weeks at a time, nothing. But the way I look at it, I'm one of the lucky ones.

JULIA. You certainly are. You made it back home.

JOHNNY. *(Completely matter-of-fact, without sentiment.)* No, I mean I'm lucky I don't remember.

> (**DAVY** *slides up behind* **JOHNNY** *and puts a drink in his hand.*)

DONNY. Say, how about this, everybody – I'm gonna change my name to Donny Nova. Tonight was the last time we get introduced with my old Polka name. From now on it's "The Donny Nova Band." Whadda ya say?

JIMMY. I can see that on a marquee.

DONNY. Darn right. Every marquee from coast to coast. It's bigger than a contest. That's why we gotta win and make the most of it. 'Cause we know, don't we, fellas? It can all be over like that. *(Snaps his fingers.)*

DAVY. One minute you're there and the next you're not.

DONNY. Right. The guys that didn't come back ain't on a marquee.

JULIA. *(Very uncomfortable.)* Like Michael?

DONNY. No, not Michael. He's...

JULIA. *(Suddenly emotional.)* Excuse me, fellas. It's late and I have to work in the morning.

> (**JULIA** *rushes to get away from the table and out of the club.)*

DONNY. No, I'm sorry –

JULIA. You were all swell tonight. A real pleasure to sing with you. I just –

DONNY. Don't go. I'm sorry –

JULIA. Nice to meet all of you. Break a leg.

> (**JULIA** *exits.)*

NICK. *(Beat. Then, abrasively.)* Who the hell's Michael?

DONNY. *(Dangerously.)* You say one ugly thing and I'll rip your face off.

NICK. I was gonna say you found a winner, but you can go to hell.

DAVY. I was gonna say the same thing. She should sing with us. Harmonies, duets maybe.

JOHNNY. But she's not a vet. There goes your gimmick.

JIMMY. She has every right to be in the band.

DONNY. Michael was her husband. He was my best friend in the thirty-seventh. He didn't make it.

> (*The scene shifts as* **DONNY** *and the* **BAND** *disappear into darkness with the Blue Wisp Jazz Club.)*

[MUSIC NO. 07B – FIRST STEPS FIRST (REPRISE)]

ENSEMBLE MEN.

IT'LL BE JUST LIKE IT WAS

Scene Seven

*(**JULIA** appears, walking on her way to work.)*

JULIA.
WHY BE ALL ALONE WHEN MUSIC CALLS?
I HAVE NOTHING MORE OR LESS TO PROVE
BUT UNLESS WE WANT A PARTY FULL
OF FLOWERS ON THE WALLS,
SOMEONE HAS TO MAKE THE VERY FIRST MOVE

*(Other **PASSERSBY** cross the space. **DONNY** appears opposite, surprising her.)*

DONNY. Hiya. I wanted to catch you before the store opened.

JULIA. I suppose I shouldn't be surprised. Look, I have to get in there, I'll be late.

DONNY. I've been waiting two hours.

JULIA. Parents warn their kids about people like you.

DONNY. Listen, I'm awfully sorry about last night.

JULIA. You did your good deed. You checked in on me and I'm fine. Time served.

DONNY. The guys loved you. You gotta admit when we found that groove, the room just lit up. There's nothin' like it. Imagine that every night. Imagine singing back up with that band.

JULIA. Is that really such a good idea?

DONNY. Davy says he can get us a gig at Oliver's Nightclub, and that's a really classy place –

JULIA. You're looking for window dressing. That department's on the sixth floor.

DONNY. Oh, a wisecracker. You might be watching too many pictures.

JULIA. Enough to know not to get myself in a no-win situation.

DONNY. Like walking in there every day to wait on a bunch of rich old ladies?

JULIA. I don't need to be rescued.

DONNY. What if I do?

>STARTING IS DAUNTING, TRUE
>TRUSTING IN SOMETHING NEW
>FEARFUL YOUR LUCK WILL BE REVERSED

>>(**DONNY** *reaches into his pocket and pulls out a folded piece of paper on which he has written his address and the time of rehearsal. He offers it to* **JULIA.**)

Come to a rehearsal tonight. If it doesn't work out I promise you'll never see my face again. If it does, it'll be a heck of a lot more exciting than singing the solo in church.

>>(**JULIA** *hesitates for a split second, then takes the piece of paper.*)

JULIA. I'll give it a try. But there are a lot of things I want to know. About Michael.

DONNY. *(Exiting.)*

>FIRST STEPS FIRST

>>(*The scene shifts as* **JULIA** *exits.*)

Scene Eight

[MUSIC NO. 08 – BREATHE]

(WAYNE and the rest of the BAND appear as the scene takes shape around DONNY. They are in mid-rehearsal at Donny's apartment.)

WAYNE. You've got a mistake in the voicing. Trombone on the third in that register is like breaking rule number one of –

DONNY. Then I'm breaking the rule, Wayne. Relax, the sky won't fall.

DAVY. *(Picking up one of WAYNE's mutes.)* Put a mute in it, Wayne.

WAYNE. *(Grabbing the mute out of DAVY's hand, genuinely irritated.)* Don't touch my stuff with your sweaty hands.

DAVY. What germs are gonna survive in my sweat? It's forty proof!

DONNY. Come on, guys. Do those bars. Everyone. Two, three, four...

> *(The BAND plays the four bars in question. It sounds perfect.)*

HALLELUJAH!
SO JUST
BREATHE
THROUGH THE INSTRUMENT,
BREATHE
THROUGH THE END OF THE PHRASE
AND AS EV'RYONE PLAYS
IT GETS EASIER
EASIER

> *(The scene continues to shift around them as JULIA appears and joins the rehearsal.)*

DONNY. It's good but watch out on "proud and tall," you're making it minor and it should be major. *(Spoken in rhythm.)* You're doing:
PROUD AND TALL

DONNY. *(Spoken in rhythm.)* And it should be:
> PROUD AND TALL
> *(Spoken in rhythm.)* You hear it?

JULIA.
> PROUD AND TALL

DONNY. *(Spoken in rhythm.)* Yeah, again.

JULIA.
> PROUD AND TALL

DONNY. *(Spoken in rhythm.)* With me.

DONNY & JULIA.
> PROUD AND TALL

DONNY. *(Spoken in rhythm.)* That's it!

> *(The scene continues to shift. **DAVY**, now obviously inebriated, falls off his stool, barely catching himself in an impressive use of his bass as a crutch.)*

Whoa! Whoa! Careful buddy!

DAVY. *(Referencing the drink he's miraculously managed not to spill a drop of.)* I got it, I got it, I got it. Disaster averted. That's why I chose the bass – holds me up when I'm half crocked.

JULIA. We're gonna break soon, how 'bout a pot of coffee?

> *(**JULIA** exits.)*

DONNY. Now when you guys play those stabs at the end, can we jump on that syncopation?

JOHNNY. They should have choreography there. Horn-ography!

DAVY. I hear Nick gives lessons.

NICK. Piss off.

DAVY.
> IT'S A GOOD THING YOU'RE ONE OF THE BEST

DAVY, WAYNE & NICK.
> BECAUSE PUTTING UP WITH YOU
> IS AN ENDURANCE TEST

DONNY.

BUT I KNOW THAT ALL THIS
IS WORTH ALL THE SWEAT

DONNY, JOHNNY & JIMMY.

BECAUSE WHEN WE'RE NAMED THE WINNERS
WE WILL FIN'LLY GET

DONNY, JOHNNY, JIMMY & WAYNE.

TO HAVE

WAYNE.

ORDER OUT OF CHAOS

DAVY.

AND MONEY TO BURN

NICK.

NO MORE NEED FOR TEACHING

JIMMY.

THE PROMISED RETURN

JIMMY & JOHNNY.

TO LIFE THE WAY IT WAS

WAYNE, NICK, JOHNNY, DAVY, JIMMY & DONNY.

AND WE CAN HAVE THIS ALL BECAUSE
I LOOK TO MY LEFT
AND LOOK TO MY RIGHT
AND SEE OTHER GUYS
WHO FIGHT THE SAME FIGHT
AND DURING THOSE FEW
SHORT HOURS A DAY
THE NOISE IN MY HEAD GOES AWAY
AND I BREATHE THROUGH THE INSTRUMENT,
BREATHE THROUGH THE END OF THE PHRASE
AND AS EV'RYONE PLAYS
IT GETS EASIER

> *(Club* **PATRONS** *emerge as Oliver's Nightclub assembles itself, with the piano, drums, and bass appearing to be on the small cabaret stage of the club.* **OLIVER** *enters.)*

[MUSIC NO. 09 – YOU DESERVE IT]

OLIVER. Swing into Oliver's!

> (**WAYNE**, **JIMMY**, *and* **NICK** *each appear in sequence playing a Reveille Fanfare as the other* **BAND MEMBERS** *take their places. At last,* **DONNY** *slides onto his piano bench as* **JULIA** *takes her place at the side of the piano.*)

DONNY.
> PICK UP THE TEMPO,
> JAZZ UP THE BEAT!
> KICK UP THE BAND,
> TICKER TAPE IN THE STREET!
> TAKE TO THE FLOOR
> NOW DON'T BE DISCREET!
> SOLDIER CUT LOOSE
> GO AND GRAB SOMEONE SWEET

DONNY & JULIA.
> 'CAUSE YOU DESERVE IT!

DONNY.
> GO OUT AND HAVE A BALL

DONNY & JULIA.
> 'CAUSE YOU DESERVE IT

DONNY.
> DON'T LET THE RHYTHM STALL

DONNY & JULIA.
> 'CAUSE WHEN YOU GOT THE CALL
> YOU STOOD UP PROUD AND TALL
> AND YOU DESERVE IT

DONNY.
> DON'T NEED A REASON
> DON'T NEED A RHYME

DONNY & JULIA.
> JUST GOTTA SWING,
> HAVE A HECK OF A TIME

DONNY.
> ACT LIKE TOMORROW
> AIN'T GONNA COME

DONNY & JULIA.

'CAUSE WHEN IT DOES, MAN
IT'S ONLY FOR SOME
'CAUSE YOU DESERVE IT
GO OUT AND HAVE A BALL
'CAUSE YOU DESERVE IT
DON'T LET THE RHYTHM STALL
'CAUSE WHEN YOU GOT THE CALL
YOU STOOD UP PROUD AND TALL
AND YOU DESERVE IT

DONNY.

HOW 'BOUT A BIG PARADE
YOU PAID YOUR DUES
AND WE OWE IT TO YA
AND NOW YOU GOT IT MADE
SO TAKE YOUR PEARL OF A GIRL
ON A WHIRL AND A TWIRL
TILL HER TOES START TO CURL
SINGIN' HALLELUJAH!

*(The **PATRONS** take the dance floor in a swing dance of wild abandon. The action on the dance floor suddenly seems to go into slow motion.)*

DONNY, JULIA, & BAND.

I LOOK TO MY LEFT
AND LOOK TO MY RIGHT
AND SEE OTHER GUYS
WHO FIGHT THE SAME FIGHT
I'M FEELIN' THE RUSH
I'M FEELIN' THE HIGH
I'M FEELIN' THE RULES DON'T APPLY

(The dance floor suddenly snaps back into real time.)

JULIA, DONNY & ENSEMBLE.

YOU DESERVE IT,
YOU DESERVE IT
YOU DESERVE IT,
YOU DESERVE IT

DONNY & JULIA.	ENSEMBLE.
'CAUSE WHEN YOU GOT THE CALL	OOO
YOU STOOD UP PROUD AND TALL	HOO HOO
AND YOU DESERVE IT YOU DESERVE IT	YOU DESERVE IT DESERVE IT YEAH!
'CAUSE WHEN YOU GOT THE CALL	DOO DOO DOO DOO
YOU STOOD UP	
PROUD AND TALL	DOO DOO DOO DOO
AND YOU DESERVE IT	
	BAH BA BAD DAP BAH
	BAH BA BAD DAP BAH
DOO'N DOO DOOT DOO	DOO DOO DOOT
WAH WAH WAH	WAH WAH WAH

[MUSIC NO. 09A – YOU DESERVE IT (PLAYOFF)]

(**OLIVER** *takes the stage as* **DONNY, JULIA,** *and the* **BAND** *take their bows and start to exit.*)

OLIVER. The Donny Nova Band, ladies and gentlemen! Remember you saw them here at Oliver's before they hit the big time.

(**DONNY** *leads* **JULIA** *off the bandstand and toward the bar. A* **BARTENDER** *greets them.*)

BARTENDER. Crowd sure loved the two of you.

DONNY. Thanks. How 'bout two Manhattans?

JULIA. Oh, why not.

(*The* **BARTENDER** *exits.*)

(*Teasing* **DONNY**.) I even remembered the bridge!

DONNY. You did more than that. You knocked it outta the ballpark. Feels fantastic, doesn't it?

JULIA. *(Surprised at feeling joy for the first time in years.)* It sure does.

*(**OLIVER** approaches their table.)*

OLIVER. Donny!

DONNY. Yes, sir?

OLIVER. Say, Private, that was aces. Can you do tomorrow night?

*(The **BARTENDER** serves the drinks.)*

DONNY. I have to ask the guys. And it'd be the same set –

OLIVER. Same set's fine. Ask 'em and let me know. Bob, those drinks are on the house. Have a good evening, folks.

DONNY. Thanks, Oliver.

*(**OLIVER** exits briskly.)*

JULIA. Well, now how about that!

DONNY. It was "You Deserve It" that did it. People like that one the best.

JULIA. It's got a real Duke Ellington flavor. But those surprise chords, they're a little Stan Kenton.

DONNY. *(Excited.)* How do you know about Stan Kenton?

JULIA. Michael's record collection. Well, *our* record collection.

DONNY. I should'a guessed. Say, speaking of Michael...

JULIA. *(Hopeful.)* Yes?

DONNY. You gotta admit Donny Nova has a terrific ring to it and I was just thinking –

JULIA. *(On to him. Not pleased.)* I married Michael Trojan. My name is Julia Trojan.

DONNY. Well, naturally, but what if you used your maiden name? "Julia Adams" sounds made for the pictures.

JULIA. I'm not going to change who I am.

DONNY. But it might be a distraction to some people –

JULIA. If it's a distraction it's because they're twelve-year-old boys. I've learned to live with that.

DONNY. But wouldn't it be great –

(*JULIA stands and begins to walk away from the conversation.*)

JULIA. Please don't push me –

(*DONNY follows her.*)

DONNY. Think of the record sales –

JULIA. Please stop.

(*JULIA begins to walk out of the club as DONNY pursues her.*)

DONNY. There's no reason to get upset.

JULIA. You're not hearing me.

(*The scene shifts to just outside the club.*)

DONNY. (*Not relenting.*) Think about it up on a marquee, "The Donny Nova Band featuring Julia Adams" –

(*JULIA turns on DONNY pointedly.*)

JULIA. (*A sudden strength fueled by grief.*) Michael's buried in someplace called Manila. I'll never get to Manila. I never got to say goodbye. A lot of things just vanished with no explanation. I want to know how his hands were folded in the casket, if his uniform was pressed, if his hair was combed right – a million things that keep me up at night and I don't need anything else erased. Certainly not his name.

DONNY. (*Beat. Then, conciliatory.*) Trust me, you don't ever wanna see Manila.

JULIA. (*Small beat.*) I just want answers.
(*In response to DONNY's lack of response.*) Look, it's the Donny Nova Band featuring Julia Trojan. That's the deal. Take it or leave it.

DONNY. Deal.

JULIA. (*Conciliatory.*) Let's go tell the guys we got another gig. Then you can walk me home, Donny Nova.

[MUSIC NO. 09B – YOU DESERVE IT (REPRISE)]

(*DONNY and JULIA start off. The scene shifts as Oliver's Nightclub begins to disappear.*)

Scene Nine

*(**DONNY**, **JULIA***, and* **NICK** *enter with* **DAVY***. It is later that night on the streets of Cleveland.* **DAVY** *is very drunk and happily leaning on both* **DONNY** *and* **NICK***, who are attempting to help get him home.)*

DAVY. ...So I say, "I survived mustard gas *and* pepper spray, so I guess that makes me a seasoned veteran." *(Pointing to his building.)* This is me. Julia, as much as I know you'd like to, I can put myself to bed thank you very much.

*(**DAVY** exits.)*

DONNY. *(To* **NICK***.)* What if he's like this on game day, or doesn't show at all?

NICK. I think you got bigger problems.

DONNY. That so?

NICK. You really think "You Deserve It" is a winner?

DONNY. It's a solid blues structure. Good hook. Can't go wrong with that.

NICK. I think Dwight Anson might have a better song.

DONNY. How do you know what kind of song Dwight Anson's got?

NICK. There's no rule against a side man playing in more than one band.

DONNY. I got that rule.

NICK. Look, I wanna play with you and the guys, but I need to win. Teaching barely covers my rent.

DONNY. You'd do this to your brothers?

[MUSIC NO. 09C – THERE IS A TRAIN]

NICK. Careful buddy. You don't get to judge.

DONNY. *(Lunging at* **NICK***.)* I'll knock your goddamn teeth out. See how well you play for Dwight Anson then!

JULIA. Donny stop! Please, just walk me home.

NICK. The show's in a week. I'll be on the bandstand with the best song.

(**NICK** *exits.*)

JULIA. Walk me home, Donny. Come on.

(*Memories of the battlefield threaten to close in on* **DONNY**.)

ENSEMBLE.
THERE IS A TRAIN
IT LEAVES THE STATION
AT A QUARTER AFTER FIVE

(*The scene shifts slightly as other late-night* **PASSERSBY** *cross the space. The front door of Julia's home appears.*)

DONNY. (*Mid-conversation, passionate, agitated.*) But that was Rubber.

ENSEMBLE.
THERE IS A TRAIN
THERE IS A TRAIN
THERE IS A TRAIN
THERE IS A TRAIN

DONNY. He always said, "You wait. When we make it big, we're takin' the train straight to New York. The five-fifteen to Grand Central. First class all the way." When we win the state broadcast, I bet that's exactly how they're gonna send us. The Cleveland Limited.

JULIA. I bet so.

DONNY. (*Beat.*) Who the hell am I kidding? We're up against huge big bands and we're barely a combo. One of 'em's goin' AWOL, one of 'em's gonna fall off the bandstand. Michael would've done it better. All of it.

(**JULIA** *takes a small journal out of her purse and starts flipping through the pages.*)

JULIA. It's here somewhere... Here, listen.

[MUSIC NO. 10 – WHO I WAS (REPRISE)]

JULIA. *(Reading from the journal.)* "When I was young I had no need for compass or for guide
A starry chart of instinct was imprinted here inside
And unaware that days of doubt and loss would soon begin –

> *(**DONNY** reads over her shoulder.)*

DONNY. – The one true course to follow was the one I found within."
What *is* that, Shakespeare? Davy give that to you?

JULIA. Oh, neither bard nor beard. It's me, silly.

DONNY. You really wrote that?

JULIA. They're just little poems, but writing them helps me get through it all.

DONNY. Let me see.

JULIA. Absolutely not. They're private.

DONNY. Is it a diary, or poems?

JULIA. Just poems.

DONNY. Then what's the big deal? I'll return it in the morning. C'mon, I'm a guy in need of inspiration.

JULIA. You'll make fun of them.

DONNY. I won't. Trust me.

JULIA. *(Handing him the journal.)* Don't stay up all night reading them. Get some sleep.

DONNY. Gave up on that a long time ago.

> *(**DONNY** exits. **JULIA** stands in her doorway, watching him walk into the darkness.)*

JULIA.
AND I WON'T DENY
WHEN I LOST HIM IT BROKE MY SOUL
DID I JUST TAKE A STEP T'WARD
SOMEHOW BEING WHOLE?
CLOSER TO WHO I WAS...

> *(**JULIA** exits through her doorway.)*

Scene Ten

(**DONNY** *appears at the piano in his apartment. He holds the journal of poems open, reading. He sets it on the piano like music and begins to play a few tentative notes and chords. As he does so, manifestations of fallen* **SERVICEMEN** *surround his piano, seeming to push him forward in his composition as he spins out a melody that is gradually overtaken by the sound of the full orchestra in his imagination. The light shifts to suggest the dawning of the following day.* **DONNY** *remains at the piano as the scene shifts around him so that he now appears to be sitting at the piano in Julia's living room. He plays an introductory arpeggio as* **JULIA** *enters, still adjusting the finishing touches on her outfit for the day's work, and stands beside him.* **DONNY** *hands her the music manuscript.*)

[MUSIC NO. 11 – LOVE WILL COME AND FIND ME AGAIN (PREPRISE)]

JULIA. This is one of my poems word for word.

DONNY. Just read it down with me.

DONNY & JULIA.

    ONCE UPON A TIME I WOULD WAKE

JULIA.

    BESIDE A MAN WHO WOULD MAKE
    ME FEEL LIKE NOTHING
    COULD TAKE HIM FROM ME...

      (**JULIA** *stops for a moment, overcome.*)

DONNY. It's really good, Julia.

JULIA. It's a little overwhelming.

DONNY. And this stanza here becomes the bridge, see? It's almost like a Gershwin song, you know?

(MRS. ADAMS enters, still in her morning robe, with coffee for DONNY.)

MRS. ADAMS. Gershwin's got nothing on you. But, then he's dead so, there's that.

JULIA. I don't know what to say.

DONNY. Say this can be our song for the contest.

JULIA. We have a song – "You Deserve It." And your lyrics are perfect –

DONNY. My lyrics are snappy, they're for kicks. You have honesty, you have sensitivity, you have...

MRS. ADAMS. Lady parts.

DONNY. Maybe that's it, but whatever it is, this song's better.

JULIA. But the contest's in a few days –

DONNY. And we need Nick on the bandstand with us. He'll know this one's a winner. I'll have the charts finished by tomorrow. I'll stay up all night. I'm good at that.

JULIA. But it's not about the troops.

DONNY. The hell it isn't. It's your story. What better tribute to the troops?

JULIA. It's a solo for a woman. You wouldn't even get to sing.

DONNY. It's the Donny Nova Band featuring Julia Trojan. That was the deal.

JULIA. *(Astonished.)* Singing about Michael. Doesn't that just beat all.

DONNY. I think it will. This song will get us to New York. Everything hangs on New York.

JULIA. Then it looks like we got our song.

(The scene shifts suddenly as JULIA, DONNY, and MRS. ADAMS disappear into the darkness along with Julia's sitting room.)

[MUSIC NO. 11A – DWIGHT ANSON & JEAN ANN]

Scene Eleven

(A microphone appears to one side as the stage of the Ohio Theatre begins to assemble itself. Various **MEMBERS** *of the Dwight Anson Orchestra appear in isolation. They each play an impressive solo or riff over an underscore of "I Know a Guy." The musical transition builds to an exciting finish as the set for the broadcast comes into focus.* **JEAN ANN RYAN**, *host of the contest, steps up to the microphone. She relishes the term "Local Celebrity" to its fullest definition.)*

JEAN ANN. The Dwight Anson Orchestra, ladies and gentlemen. What a sizzling tune. I can't say for sure but this contest may have just been sewn up.

> (**ROGER COHEN**, *the no-nonsense producer of the broadcast, appears to the side of the stage, script pages in hand.)*

Once again, this is Jean Ann Ryan, your host for tonight's broadcast, brought to you by Bayer Aspirin – just in time for the holidays.

> (**DONNY, DAVY, JOHNNY, JIMMY, NICK, WAYNE,** *and* **JULIA** *enter and take their place in the center of the stage, instruments at the ready.* **ROGER** *approaches* **JEAN ANN** *with script pages.)*

Our last contestants are six of our boys just home from the war and a young lady whose husband gave his life in the Pacific. With a song for all the gold star women out there, the Donny Nova Band featuring Julia Trojan.

> (**JEAN ANN** *exits.* **JULIA** *begins the song with obvious vulnerability. She is singing about a private chapter in her life. As the song progresses, she gains strength and stamina before our eyes. It is a star-making performance through its honesty.)*

[MUSIC NO. 12 – LOVE WILL COME AND FIND ME AGAIN]

JULIA.

ONCE UPON A TIME I WOULD WAKE
BESIDE A MAN WHO WOULD MAKE
ME FEEL LIKE NOTHING
COULD TAKE HIM FROM ME...
ONCE I THOUGHT FOREVER WAS REAL
I THOUGHT MY LIFE WAS IDEAL
I THOUGHT THAT NOTHING
COULD STEAL IT, YOU SEE
ONCE I LEARNED HOW WRONG I HAD BEEN
THAT SOMETIMES DREAMS CAN CAVE IN
AND WHAT THEN?
ONCE I LEARNED THE HARD WAY
FAITH IN EVER-AFTER WAS DONE
AND I GAVE UP EVER WONDERING WHEN
LOVE WILL COME AND FIND ME AGAIN

AND IT'S ALMOST LIKE TIME HAS STOOD STILL
LIKE A LIFETIME ICED UNDER A FROST
AND I DON'T TRY TO WARM FROM THE CHILL
ALTHOUGH I KNOW HOW MUCH I'VE LOST
TROUBLE IS THE MORE YOU DENY
THE MORE YOU DON'T EVEN TRY
THE MORE THE WORLD PASSES BY IN A HAZE
SOON YOU FIND YOU DON'T EVEN KNOW
HOW MANY YEARS YOU LET GO
THE CHANCES WASTED IN SO MANY WAYS
LATELY I'VE BEEN THINKING IT'S TIME
TO TAKE A LOOK AT WHAT I'M DOING THEN
CLINGING TO "IF ONLY"
HEAVEN KNOWS THERE'S MORE THAN ONE MAN
AND MAYBE I SHOULD BE PLANNING FOR WHEN
LOVE WILL COME AND FIND ME AGAIN
LETTING GO OF WHAT MIGHT HAVE BEEN
AND LETTING SOMETHING ELSE IN
ONLY THEN
LOVE WILL COME

AND FIND ME
AGAIN

> (**JEAN ANN** *returns to the stage at her microphone.* **DONNY**, **JULIA**, *and the* **BAND** *wave to the crowd.*)

JEAN ANN. Weren't they fabulous, ladies and gentlemen? And now, our judges' momentous decision.

> (**ROGER COHEN** *steps onstage and hands* **JEAN ANN** *an envelope.*)

Thank you, Roger.

[MUSIC NO. 12A – AND THE WINNER IS]

> (**ROGER** *steps to the side.*)

And the winning song that will represent the great state of Ohio is... "Love Will Come and Find Me Again" by the Donny Nova Band.

> (**DONNY**, **JULIA**, *and the entire* **BAND** *make their way back onstage.*)

Mr. Nova, would you like to say a few words?

> (**DONNY** *steps to the microphone, guiding* **JULIA** *along with him.*)

DONNY. Well, gosh, this is...this is going to change every one of our lives. For all us vets out there, we appreciate this more than we can say.

JEAN ANN. On behalf of everyone here at the beautiful Ohio Theatre, on the Rive Gauche of Lake Erie, congratulations and goodnight one and all!

[MUSIC NO. 12B – END OF BROADCAST]

ROGER. And...we're...off the air. That's it everyone. Good job, thank you all, thank you audience!

STAGEHAND. Bring in the house curtain.

> (*A light shift suggests a front house curtain descends and those onstage are no longer visible to the audience.*)

ROGER. Well done, Jean.

JEAN ANN. *(Virtually weeping.)* Such an honor, truly, Roger.

> *(**JEAN ANN** exits. **ROGER** motions to a **STAFF**
> **PHOTOGRAPHER**.)*

ROGER. Bobby, could you take their picture? Fellas, get together there, closer, that's it. Big smiles.

> *(The **STAFF PHOTOGRAPHER** takes a picture of
> them.)*

Perfect. Mr. Nova, congratulations. I'm Roger Cohen, producer. Let me go over a few things with you right away.

DONNY. Yes, sir.

> *(**DONNY**, **JULIA**, and the **BAND** move with
> **ROGER** out of the way of **STAGEHANDS**
> beginning to clear the bandstand.)*

ROGER. Now here are the papers that explain everything that will happen in New York, rules, time restrictions, and so forth. Two things are most important: the broadcast is Sunday, December sixteenth, but there's a preliminary off-air on Wednesday the twelfth to determine which bands make the broadcast.

DONNY. A preliminary? Wasn't *this* the preliminary for New York?

ROGER. It's only a two hour program, Mr. Nova.

JULIA. Wait a minute –

ROGER. *(Dismissing her.)* Sweetie... Furthermore, you're responsible for travel and accommodation expenses for any and all personnel, whether on-air or support staff.

DAVY. What?

DONNY. We have to pay for everything?

ROGER. Yes.

DONNY. Even if we go cheap it's gonna be close to a grand. We don't have that kinda money.

JOHNNY. Nobody does. Who can afford that?

JIMMY. Listen, the *public* believes all forty-eight states are being represented. That's just not what you're selling.

ROGER. What are you, the *Legal*?

JIMMY. As a matter of fact –

ROGER. What we're selling is Bayer Aspirin, in case you didn't notice.

NICK. I fought Hitler so you can sell aspirin?

ROGER. This isn't about you.

DONNY. "American Songbook's Tribute to the Troops." *We're* the troops!

ROGER. Actually, you're just a contestant. And you have until Friday, November sixteenth to call NBC to confirm, or forfeit your appearance.

JIMMY. We should at least be entitled to travel reimbursement –

ROGER. What you think you're entitled to might not be compatible with broadcasting a nationwide music contest with enough time to sell –

DAVY. Bayer fucking Aspirin!

ROGER. Watch it, pal. If you're not happy with the opportunity we're handing you, we'll give it to the runner-up. New York won't know the difference.

DONNY. Everyone just heard us win.

ROGER. Who? A couple of folks in Cleveland? Come on, kid. Rule number one: If no one saw it, it didn't happen.

> (*A shock wave seems to hit each of the* **BAND MEMBERS** *like a bullet.* **DONNY** *disengages, struggling to process his emotions.* **JULIA** *notices and keeps a concerned eye on him.*)

WAYNE. So if by some miracle we raise the money in time, we gotta call you to say we're gonna pay our own way there, put ourselves up and we still gotta audition with no guarantee we'll even be on the broadcast?

> (**JIMMY** *reaches to calm him down.*)

> (*In a violent outburst.*) Don't touch me!

ROGER. I don't make the rules.

DAVY. Well, who does? 'Cause maybe they take suggestions. Like throwing us out a plane and seeing how many make it *parachuting* in. Or a three day march. Hey, it's winter – so we lose a few toes.

JOHNNY. Not askin' much. We dig our own latrines.

WAYNE. Don't need clean water.

[MUSIC NO. 12C – DIRTY WATER]

DAVY. What's a little dysentery among friends.

JOHNNY. *(Moving in on* **ROGER**.*)* You remember that, right? You were there, right?

DAVY. Or were you in your fuckin' corner office?

ROGER. *(Thrusting the paper at* **JIMMY**.*)* This copy is yours. Again, congratulations. It's a swell tune.

   (**ROGER** *exits swiftly.*)

DAVY. *(Attempting gallows humor.)* How many bottles is it gonna take to make this all go away?

WAYNE. *(Darker.)* I can think of something quicker. It never ends!

> (**DONNY**, **JULIA**, *and the* **BAND** *are left on a half-disassembled stage with a few disinterested* **STAGEHANDS** *cleaning far upstage. There is the sound of a powerful explosion representing the collective traumatic memories of everyone in the band. They are all lost in isolation for a brief moment. The rhythm of* **DONNY***'s determination rises – a tom-tom swing pattern, low and dangerous.)*

[MUSIC NO. 13 – RIGHT THIS WAY]

JULIA. Donny...?

DONNY.
  THERE IS A TRAIN
  IT LEAVES THE STATION
  AT A QUARTER AFTER FIVE
  AND IT'S DIRECT

FROM UNION TERMINAL
RIGHT THERE IN PUBLIC SQUARE
A QUARTER AFTER FIVE
AND WHERE DOES IT ARRIVE?
AT GRAND CENTRAL STATION!

THE CLEVELAND LIMITED
OF NEW YORK CENTRAL RAILROAD
HAS FIRST-CLASS PULLMAN CARS
FOR BIG TIME MOVIE STARS
AND WE'RE GONNA TAKE ONE
I SEE IT ALL
THE LEATHER SEAT,
THE STEAK WE'LL EAT,
AND THEN THAT TRAIN CONDUCTOR'S CALL

HE'LL SAY, "RIGHT THIS WAY
WE'VE RESERVED THIS JUST FOR YOU
YOU'VE BEEN WAITING FOR THIS DAY
IT'S THE LEAST THAT WE CAN DO
LET ME TAKE YOUR BAGS MY FRIEND
YOU'VE BEEN CARRYING THOSE FAR TOO LONG
TROUBLED TIMES ARE AT AN END
AND WE'RE WAITING TO HEAR YOUR SONG
IT'S A PRIV'LEGE, SIR, MAY I SAY
RIGHT THIS WAY"

AND IN TIMES SQUARE
THE HOTEL ASTOR
STANDS ELEVEN STORIES HIGH
A FIRST-CLASS GRAND HOTEL
THE LOBBY'S IN A MOVIE
THAT I SAW LAST MONTH AS WELL
WITH GARLAND AND WALKER
AND ON THE TOP
A ROOFTOP GARDEN
WITH A BANDSTAND IN THE SKY

CREAM OF THE CROP
WHERE DORSEY SWINGS
AND ELLA SINGS

AND I SWEAR SOME DAY SO WILL I

THEY'LL SAY, "RIGHT THIS WAY
WE'VE RESERVED THIS JUST FOR YOU
YOU'VE BEEN WAITING FOR THIS DAY
IT'S THE LEAST THAT WE CAN DO
YOU'VE ARRIVED AT LAST, MY FRIEND
YOU'VE BEEN FIGHTING FOR FAR TOO LONG"
AFTER BUNKS ON CARGO SHIPS,
AFTER TRENCHES IN THE RAIN,
AFTER RUNNING FOR COVER,
WHILE DODGING THE FLACK
AND THREE YEARS AND EIGHT MONTHS
TO FIGHT MY WAY BACK,

DONNY & BAND.

AND LOSING MY FAITH

DONNY.

WHILE BUSTING MY ASS…

(Beat.)

I THINK WE'RE ENTITLED
TO TRAVEL FIRST-CLASS.

Don't you?

WAYNE. How?

DONNY.

WHATEVER GIGS,
WHATEVER DATES,
WHATEVER BOOKINGS WE CAN GET
WE TAKE 'EM ALL
IF THERE'S A CLUB IN TOWN
WHERE WE CAN PLAY A SET
WE ARE NOT FINISHED YET

DAVY.

THERE'S LIQUOR DIVES,

JOHNNY.

AND PARTY ROOMS,

WAYNE.

AND V.A. HALLS I BET

DONNY. Right!

DONNY & BAND.

    WE FIGHT FOR OURSELVES NOW

DONNY.

    AND ALL OF THE WRONGS

    WILL BE MADE RIGHT THIS WAY!

BAND.

    WE'LL HEAR, "RIGHT THIS WAY"

DONNY.

    "RIGHT THIS WAY"

BAND.

    AFTER ALL THAT WE'VE BEEN THROUGH

DONNY.

    WHAT WE'VE BEEN THROUGH

BAND.

    WE'VE BEEN WAITING

BAND.	**DONNY.**
FOR THIS DAY	WE'VE BEEN
IT'S THE LEAST THAT	WAITING
THEY CAN DO	

WAYNE & JOHNNY.

    AT LAST

DONNY, JIMMY, NICK & DAVY.

    WE'VE ARRIVED AT LAST,

DONNY & BAND.

    MY FRIEND

    WE'VE BEEN FIGHTING FOR FAR TOO LONG

DONNY, JULIA & BAND.

    TROUBLED TIMES ARE AT AN END

    AND THEY'RE WAITING TO HEAR OUR SONG

    YOU CAN BET WE INTEND TO STAY

    RIGHT THIS WAY!

ACT II

Scene One

[MUSIC NO. 14 – ENTR'ACTE]

(**DONNY, JULIA, WAYNE, JOHNNY, DAVY, JIMMY,** *and* **NICK** *appear out of the darkness. We see each one in their own time and space preparing for another performance to raise the money to get to New York.*)

[MUSIC NO. 15 – NOBODY]

DONNY.
YOU KNOW WHO TELLS ME "NO"?
YOU KNOW WHO TELLS ME
"I DON'T THINK SO"?
YOU KNOW WHO TELLS ME "NO"?
NOBODY

WAYNE.
YOU KNOW WHO TELLS ME "WAIT"?

NICK.
YOU KNOW WHO TELLS ME
"THAT AIN'T SO GREAT"?

WAYNE.
YOU KNOW WHO TELLS ME "WAIT"?

WAYNE, NICK & DONNY.
NOBODY

WAYNE, NICK, DONNY & ENSEMBLE MEN.
SO GET OUTTA MY WAY

DAVY.
'SPECIALLY IF YOU DON'T HAVE
SOMETHING NICER TO SAY

WAYNE, NICK, DONNY & ENSEMBLE MEN.
> GO TRY TO BREAK
> SOMEONE OTHER!

DAVY.
> GO FIND YOURSELF
> SOMEONE ELSE TO SMOTHER

ENSEMBLE MEN.
> NO OOOH, NOBODY NO

JULIA.	**MRS. ADAMS.**
YOU KNOW WHO TELLS ME "SLOW"?	OOH, SLOW
YOU KNOW WHO TELLS ME "THAT'S A NO-GO"?	OOH AH THAT'S A NO-GO
YOU KNOW WHO TELLS ME "SLOW"?	OOH, SLOW

JULIA, MRS. ADAMS & ENSEMBLE.
> NOBODY

JOHNNY.
> YOU KNOW WHO TELLS ME "QUIT"?

JIMMY.
> YOU KNOW WHO TELLS ME

JIMMY & ENSEMBLE WOMEN.
> "YOU AIN'T WORTH SPIT"?

JOHNNY.
> YOU KNOW WHO TELLS ME "QUIT"?

JULIA, JIMMY, JOHNNY & ENSEMBLE.
> NOBODY

JULIA & ENSEMBLE.
> SO GET OUTTA MY WAY!

DONNY, JULIA & ENSEMBLE.
> FIND SOMEBODY ELSE
> WHO GIVES A FIG WHAT YOU SAY

JULIA, BAND & ENSEMBLE.
> GO DISCIPLINE SOMEONE OTHER!
> LAST TIME I CHECKED
> YOU WERE NOT MY MOTHER
> YOU KNOW WHO TELLS ME "STOP"?

YOU KNOW WHO TELLS ME
"YOU DON'T HAVE WHAT IT TAKES
AND YOU WILL NEVER REACH THE TOP"?
YOU KNOW WHO TELLS ME "STOP"?
NOBODY!

> *(We see their various vignettes ultimately coalesce onto the stage of the Pavilion Nightclub.* **DANCING COUPLES** *take to the dance floor and mingle at tables in front of the* **BAND** *as they blast an instrumental break.)*

DONNY & JULIA.
SO GET OUTTA MY WAY!
FIND SOMEBODY ELSE
WHO GIVES A FIG WHAT YOU SAY
GO DISCIPLINE SOMEONE OTHER
LAST TIME I CHECKED
YOU WERE NOT MY MOTHER!

DONNY, JULIA & ENSEMBLE.
YOU KNOW WHO TELLS ME "STOP"?
YOU KNOW WHO TELLS ME
"YOU DON'T HAVE WHAT IT TAKES
AND YOU WILL NEVER REACH THE TOP"?
YOU KNOW WHO TELLS ME "STOP"?

JULIA.
NOBODY

DONNY & JULIA.
NOBODY

DONNY, JULIA, BAND &
   ENSEMBLE WOMEN.

DONNY, JULIA, BAND & ENSEMBLE WOMEN.	ENSEMBLE MEN.
NO, NO ONE TELLS ME NO	NO, NO
	NO

DONNY & ENSEMBLE GROUP 1.	
NO ONE TELLS ME	**JULIA & ENSEMBLE GROUP 2.**
	NO ONE TELLS ME
NO ONE TELLS ME	
	NO ONE TELLS ME

ENSEMBLE MEN.	ENSEMBLE WOMEN.	DONNY & JULIA.
NO (NO) (NO)BODY	NO NO (NO)BODY	NOBODY

[MUSIC NO. 16 – THE BOYS ARE BACK]

(The **DANCING COUPLES** *cross the space as the scene begins to shift.)*

ENSEMBLE. *(Spoken in rhythm.)* The boys are back.

The boys are back.

The boys are back.

The boys are back.

Oh ah!

The boys are back.

The boys are back.

THEY'RE GOIN' TO NEW YORK

*(***DAVY** *and* **JOHNNY** *perform a duet on* **DAVY***'s bass.)*

Scene Two

(The scene shifts to Donny's apartment. **DONNY** *sits at his piano working on music charts.* **JULIA** *stands next to him.)*

DONNY. Now I've already started the intro chords but Rubber looks out at all these troops, and he knows they need something to pick 'em up, not a sappy ballad. So he starts taking off – tst-t-t-tst-t-t-tt-t-tst– and I look at him and he says, "Faster!" And then he bumps it up again and says, "Faster!" And he kicks it up again and yells, "Now sing!" And I start singing like my life depends on it and it's not a love song anymore, it's I don't know, a battle call or something. I swear, he turned that camp into the bandstand on the top of the New Amsterdam.

JULIA. That must've been something.

DONNY. Say, when's your father back in town? Be nice to put him on a guest list. Maybe the big booth at the Pavilion.

JULIA. I'll check. Where do we stand on the "Help-Sell-Bayer-Aspirin" Fund?

DONNY. Well, Pullman Car train tickets for all of us and rooms at the Astor for that long are gonna run two-thousand, two-hundred. We only got three gigs lined up this week.

JULIA. But we're going to need at least five or six a week to make it.

DONNY. I went down to my dad's old factory yesterday to see if I could pick up a few hours.

JULIA. That's a terrific idea.

DONNY. Except all those fellas see me on stage, think I'm really something –

JULIA. Those fellas think you're something because you're one of them. Cleveland's own.

*(**JULIA** picks up a ukulele and strums a chord as she sings a spontaneous melody.)*

[MUSIC NO. 18 – I GOT A THEORY]

JULIA.

I GOT A THEORY,
WHEN YOU ARE FROM LAKE ERIE
YOU'RE BETTER THAN THE AV'RAGE JOE

> (**DONNY** *plays a chord on the piano and sings along with the improvisation.*)

DONNY.

THOUGH BURIED IN SNOW

JULIA.

IT'S TIME TO LET THE WHOLE WORLD KNOW

> (**DONNY** *plays an even more elaborate accompaniment.*)

DONNY.

I GOT A THEORY,

JULIA.

IT TAKES A PLACE THIS DREARY
TO GIVE A GUY THE RIGHT AMOUNT

DONNY.

OF DRIVE TO SURMOUNT

JULIA.

IT'S TIME TO TELL THE WORLD WE COUNT

DONNY. I think we're on to something here.

JULIA. *(Thrilled.)* Yeah, keep writing. With this one we might get more gigs than we need.

> (*The scene shifts as* **DONNY** *and* **JULIA** *disappear into darkness.*)

ENSEMBLE.

I GOT A THEORY,
WHEN YOU ARE FROM LAKE ERIE
YOU'RE BETTER THAN THE AV'RAGE JOE
THOUGH BURIED IN SNOW,
IT'S TIME TO LET THE WHOLE WORLD KNOW

SHRINER.	ENSEMBLE.
The Al Koran Shriners welcome the Donny Nova Band!	BA DOOT DAH BA DOOT DAH I'M GONNA HEAR MY BAND AT EIGHT

(*DANCING COUPLES cross through the space.* **NICK** *and* **WAYNE** *appear, packing up their instruments after the gig. They are unaware* **JULIA** *is in the background. She overhears their conversation.*)

NICK. I just heard an old friend in Chicago is in the band that won for Illinois.

WAYNE. They gonna go?

NICK. Hell, yeah. He's loaded, and we're still nowhere near.

WAYNE. We've still got time.

NICK. Hey, aren't you running late? Your wife'll fall to pieces if you're off your schedule.

WAYNE. Well, that's the thing. I guess she fell to pieces *because* of my schedule. I forget they're not my troops. Can't run a household like a platoon. I've been staying at the Hotel Euclid for the past week.

NICK. Shit, Lieutenant, I'm sorry to hear that.

WAYNE. Oh, gimme a break. You're loving this.

NICK. (*Beat.*) Get your things and come to my place.

WAYNE. No –

NICK. Consider that an order, you screwy nutcase.

(**WAYNE** *and* **NICK** *start off.*)

You keep things spotless, right?

WAYNE. What do you think?

NICK. I think I just got a live-in maid.

(**NICK** *and* **WAYNE** *exit as the scene shifts and* **JULIA** *fades into darkness.*)

ENSEMBLE MEN.

    WHEN JOHN D,   **ENSEMBLE WOMEN.**

    THAT OLD ROCKEFELLER   UH HUH

    FIRST SET FOOT

    ON CLEVELAND SOIL   ON CLEVELAND SOIL

    NO ONE THOUGHT HE

        WAS

    ANYTHING STELLAR   UH UH

ENSEMBLE.

    THEN HE STRUCK IT

    WITH STANDARDIZED OIL

    (Spoken in rhythm.) It gives us our aroma!

        (The lights change as Oliver's Nightclub appears. It is just before opening. **DONNY** *is at the piano.* **JULIA** *and the rest of the* **BAND** *begin to assemble around him.* **WAYNE** *has a copy of* The Plain Dealer *newspaper.* **OLIVER** *enters near the bar, unseen by* **DONNY, JULIA,** *and the* **BAND.***)*

WAYNE. How about today's *Plain Dealer*? Full-page ad.

DONNY. Let me see.

        (**WAYNE** *opens up the paper to show everyone.)*

WAYNE. *(Reading.)* "For faster pain relief the Donny Nova Band demands genuine Bayer Aspirin."

JIMMY. That's the picture they took at the contest.

JOHNNY. I forget a lot of stuff, but I think I would remember getting paid for that.

JIMMY. And without our permission. That's...irksome.

NICK. No, that's *shitty*. Irksome is your use of the word irksome.

JULIA. While we're scrounging for every penny...

WAYNE. We only got, what, not even half the money raised yet?

        (**OLIVER** *stops for a moment, eavesdropping.)*

So what's plan B? Greyhound Bus? Stay at the "Y"?

DONNY. Not if I can help it.

JIMMY. But with no on-air guarantee, why spend the money? What about driving?

JOHNNY. Driving to New York in the winter? Do you know what it's like to have a car flip –

WAYNE, JIMMY, DAVY, NICK & DONNY. Three times, we know, three times.

> (**OLIVER** *loudly clears his throat as he approaches them.*)

OLIVER. Getting ready for the big trip next month?

DONNY. Sure thing.

OLIVER. *(Testing the waters.)* Hope the weather doesn't make getting there tough.

DONNY. Oh, NBC's sending us on the Cleveland Limited. Pullman Cars.

JIMMY. That's right.

OLIVER. Jeez, how 'bout that. That must be costing them a fortune.

DONNY. It's the least they could do.

OLIVER. That's good to hear. Say, I had a band cancel on me, so can I book you guys again for tomorrow night? I know it's last-minute, and you'd be savin' my butt, so how 'bout I toss in an extra fifty.

DONNY. *(Trying to play it cool.)* Guys?

OLIVER. I'm really in a bind – make it an extra seventy-five.

DONNY. *(Trying even harder to play it cool.)* I suppose we could –

OLIVER. You drive a hard bargain, kid. Hundred extra, that's the best I can do. Help a guy out.

DONNY. *(Just short of flabbergasted.)* Sure thing. We can do that for you, Oliver. Tomorrow night.

OLIVER. Swell. Break a leg tonight.

> (**OLIVER** *exits, pleased with himself and thinking of a plan.*)

DONNY. Johnny, what's that bring the total to?

JOHNNY. *(Does a quick rhythmic tapping pattern against his chest.)* Nine-hundred and thirty-six dollars and seventy-eight cents.

WAYNE. How do you do that?

JOHNNY. I have no idea.

> *(The scene shifts to a live WTAM broadcast with* **JEAN ANN RYAN.***)*

JOHNNY.	**WAYNE, NICK & DAVY.**
WHEN BOB HOPE WAS ONLY	OOO
	DOOT
CALLED "LESTER"	DOOT
A BUSKER	DOOT DOOT
IN OLD LUNA PARK	HE STARTED OUT AS
WHO'DA GUESSED THAT	A BUSKER
THAT POOR LITTLE JESTER	DOOT DOOT DOOT

JOHNNY, WAYNE, DAVY & NICK.
IN THE MOVIES WOULD MAKE SUCH A MARK?!

JEAN ANN. Cleveland's crème de la crème taking New York by storm in just three weeks!

> *(***OLIVER** *appears in his own time and space, phone in hand.)*

OLIVER. Jo? It's Oliver. I need your help with something. It's about the Donny Nova Band.

> *(***JO** *appears in her own time and space, phone in hand.)*

JO. Al? It's Jo. Oliver called. Now don't give me any of your crap, you're gonna help me out with the Donny Nova Band.

ENSEMBLE.
I GOT A THEORY
THAT PEOPLE FROM LAKE ERIE
HAVE PLENTY MORE TO BRAG ABOUT
THERE'S TALENT, NO DOUBT
IT'S TIME TO LET THE SECRET OUT

> *(***DANCING COUPLES*** cross the space. The lights change as* **DAVY** *and* **JULIA** *are revealed at a table at the Pavilion Nightclub.)*

DAVY. You just sang a very good set, my dear. *(Motioning for a waiter.)* Hey, buddy? A whiskey.

WAITER. Coming right up, Mr. Zlatic.

JULIA. Ever thought of giving up the bottle?

DAVY. Listen, I'm not suffering from what some people call alcoholism. I'm loving every minute of it.

JULIA. I'm being serious.

DAVY. *(As serious as he will ever be.)* Julia, even though there isn't enough whiskey in the world to wash away what I saw in those camps, I owe it to myself to try. "Let that suffice, most forcible Feeble."

> *(The* **WAITER** *delivers the drink, then exits.)*

Thanks, buddy.

> *(***DAVY*** drinks his whiskey as the lights shift away from the table and the* **DANCING COUPLES** *move to obscure it from view.)*

AL.	DANCING COUPLES.
Cleveland's finest! Back at the Pavilion.	DOO

JO.	
From the Blue Wisp to the big time!	DOO

JEAN ANN.	
Back by popular demand, the Donny Nova Band!	DOO

OLIVER.	
Tonight at Oliver's, you know who!	I WANNA HEAR MY FAV'RITE SONG

DANCING COUPLES.
  I WANNA HEAR MY BAND
  AT EIGHT

(**DONNY** *and the* **BAND** *appear center, as
the lighting suggests the stage of Oliver's
Nightclub.*)

DONNY, JULIA & CLUB PATRONS.

I GOT A THEORY
WE GET A LITTLE WEARY
OF PEOPLE DUMPIN' ON THIS TOWN
IT'S TRUE THAT THE

DONNY. *(Spoken in rhythm.)* Winters are endless

JULIA. *(Spoken in rhythm.)* The lake is polluted

DONNY. *(Spoken in rhythm.)* The ball team is losing

JULIA. *(Spoken in rhythm.)* The sewers exploded

DONNY. *(Spoken in rhythm.)* The mob is returning

JULIA & BAND. *(Spoken in rhythm.)* The river's on fire again!

JULIA, DONNY & CLUB PATRONS.

BUT NOTHIN'S GONNA KEEP US DOWN!

JULIA.

THEY GOT THEIR FANCY ACCENTS
ON THE EAST SIDE OF MANHATTAN

DONNY, JIMMY, NICK & ENSEMBLE MEN.

BUT WE AIN'T MET A VOWEL WE COULDN'T FIND
A WAY TO FLATTEN

DONNY.

THE VANDERBILTS MAY SUMMER
AT THE SPA IN SARATOGA

JULIA & ENSEMBLE WOMEN.

BUT NOTHIN' BEATS THE WATERS
OF THE FLAMING CUYAHOGA!

JULIA, DONNY & ENSEMBLE.

I GOT A THEORY
IF GOD ABOVE CAN HEAR HE
IS SWINGIN' TO THESE TUNES OF OURS
BREAK OUT THE CIGARS
'CAUSE CLEVELAND'S GOT SOME
BRAND NEW STARS

(**JOHNNY** *plays a drum solo and ends by saying:*)

JOHNNY. We love you, Cleveland!

JULIA, DONNY & ENSEMBLE.

YEAH

(*The* **ENSEMBLE** *applauds the end of the number and gathers excitedly around the* **BAND.** *The scene shifts as Oliver's Nightclub disappears into the darkness.*)

[MUSIC NO. 18A – I GOT A THEORY (PLAYOFF)]

Scene Three

(**DONNY** *and* **JULIA** *step out of the darkness. They begin to stroll along as if on the sidewalks of downtown Cleveland.*)

DONNY. It turned colder.

JULIA. The streetcar will be here soon.

DONNY. Say, have you told your boss you'll need that week off at work?

JULIA. Oh, yes.

DONNY. And he's okay with it?

JULIA. Sure. It just means I'll no longer be working there.

DONNY. What are you talking about?

JULIA. He said I had to make a choice between taking time off and the security of my position.

DONNY. Julia, no –

JULIA. Everything happens for a reason. I'll grab all the overtime I can and as many lipsticks as I can fit in my unmentionables on my way out.

DONNY. After we win this thing, you won't need that lousy job anyway.

JULIA. But what if we don't even make it on the program?

DONNY. We will.

JULIA. What if we don't win.

DONNY. We will.

JULIA. Yeah, but what if we *don't*?

DONNY. Then I guess you can sell Frigidaires with your father.

JULIA. My father doesn't sell Frigidaires.

DONNY. *(Beat.)* Go on.

JULIA. He sells insurance and lives in an apartment with his secretary about, ooooohh, maybe six blocks down that way.

DONNY. I don't know what to say.

JULIA. You don't have to say anything. I just wanted to be honest.

DONNY. Thanks.

JULIA. I want *you* to be honest.

DONNY. About what?

JULIA. You said you were there. I'm tired of waiting. I just want to know.

DONNY. *(Beginning to feel panicked.)* He died Julia, what else is there to say?

JULIA. *Everything*. Was it quick? Did he suffer? Was he trying to save someone?

DONNY. *(Desperate.)* Stop it – you don't want to know.

JULIA. *(Forcefully.)* For a year and a half that's *all* I've wanted to know. Was he scared? What was the last thing he said? Were his eyes open?

DONNY. *(Exploding.)* There were no eyes! Jesus Christ, it's not like the movies. Okay, Julia? It's just not like the movies. There was no face, no hair to comb, no hands to fold. Just stop it.

JULIA. *(Wounded, but determined – almost a threat.)* I'm still waiting.

DONNY. *(Long beat.)* "Hill 700" was this big hill we needed to keep from the Japs. Michael and I were in a trench on the side of the hill, going on three days without sleep. There were these pillboxes above us, bunkers, and they'd just fire down at us and we were trapped. So that night it starts raining and Michael says one way or another we gotta try to make some headway – toss some grenades, then make a run at them or fall back. So Michael throws first and it must have gotten pretty close because they start firing down again. It's dark and they're firing and it's raining and I have my grenade in my hand and I pull the pin and my grenade drops –

JULIA. Don't say any more –

DONNY. Just right into the mud and I know the spoon's released now and I start reaching for it and I can't see it and Michael's reaching around down there trying to grab it and I say, "Get out" and I jump out and roll down the hill and I know he has to be behind me, he *has* to be 'cause I said to get out.

JULIA. Please stop.

DONNY. And I roll into a foxhole and I feel it go off.

JULIA. Stop talking.

DONNY. And he wasn't next to me where I thought he'd be and I crawled back up there and it was just black. And I sat back down in that pit all night and tried to keep the rain from washing things away...getting in the mud...

(**JULIA** *walks away from* **DONNY**.)

Julia, wait –

JULIA. No.

DONNY. *(Broken.)* I'm sorry.

JULIA. Donny, just go home. For God's sake go home, Donny.

(**JULIA** *rushes off into the darkness.* **DONNY** *stands under the light of the streetcar stop for a moment. The scene begins to shift.*)

Scene Four

(Center, behind **DONNY**, *appear* **JIMMY**, **DAVY**, **NICK**, **WAYNE**, *and* **JOHNNY**. *They are in a greenroom area that appears to be just offstage at a new supper club. A nervous female* **ENTERTAINMENT DIRECTOR** *approaches them.* **WAYNE** *is obsessively polishing the bell of his trombone.)*

ENTERTAINMENT DIRECTOR.	DAVY.
I don't know how much longer we can wait. The guests were told you'd begin at seven and it's already seven-fifteen.	*(To* **JIMMY**.*)* Do you think she forgot?

*(**DONNY** crosses and enters the greenroom.)*

WAITER. Table four just sent back the chicken.

JOHNNY. Another bus went by and she wasn't on it.

ENTERTAINMENT DIRECTOR. Mr. Nova, we have a full house tonight –

DONNY. Can I use your phone?

ENTERTAINMENT DIRECTOR. *(Pointing out a telephone on a small side table in the room.)* Certainly. Now, you'll open with "Love Will Come and Find Me," the contest song, right?

*(**DONNY** picks up the phone.)*

JIMMY. We like to save that one for the end, just to remind everyone to listen to the big broadcast coming up.

ENTERTAINMENT DIRECTOR. Well, if they're not all asleep by then. It's really getting late…

DONNY. *(Into the phone.)* Plaza-seven-two-three-six-eight please.

(On the far side of the space a telephone rings.)

JIMMY. Then sure, we'll open with "Love Will Come and Find Me," that's fine.

*(**MRS. ADAMS** enters on the far side of the space as if into her kitchen. She picks up the ringing telephone.)*

MRS. ADAMS. Hello?

DONNY. Mrs. Adams?

MRS. ADAMS. Yes?

DONNY. It's Donny Novitski. Is Julia there?

MRS. ADAMS. Well, you see –

DONNY. We're supposed to go on at Lakewood Supper Club –

ENTERTAINMENT DIRECTOR. Twenty minutes ago.

DONNY. Is she on her way?

MRS. ADAMS. I'm so sorry, Donny, but she's come down with a terrible... Well she's very sick and it came on suddenly.

DONNY. Is she there?

MRS. ADAMS. She wanted to call but we didn't have the number for the new club, see, and –

DONNY. Let me speak to her.

MRS. ADAMS. She really can't get out of bed, dear. I'm so sorry.

DONNY. Please –

MRS. ADAMS. She'll call when she's better, I'll make sure of it.

DONNY. *(Beat.)* Alright then.

MRS. ADAMS. Goodbye, dear.

*(**DONNY** hangs up the phone. **MRS. ADAMS** remains standing in her kitchen.)*

DONNY. Let's just play the gig.

ENTERTAINMENT DIRECTOR. And Mrs. Trojan?

DONNY. She's ill. I'll be singing everything tonight. Let's go, fellas.

[MUSIC NO. 18B – WHERE'S JULIA]

WAYNE. *(Quietly panicking.)* Is she out? What's that mean for New York?

JOHNNY. We're not gonna go? You mean we can't go?

> *(The **ENTERTAINMENT DIRECTOR** leads them off, exiting toward the stage, as the center greenroom area disappears into the darkness. **JULIA** steps out into the light of the kitchen beside **MRS. ADAMS**.)*

MRS. ADAMS. Your father used to have people do that to me – call and lie for him.

JULIA. I'm sorry.

MRS. ADAMS. As bad as what you or I have been through, it's nothing compared to what he has. He made a promise to Michael to look after you. He kept his promise. You made a promise to that band to show up and sing. Your father probably told me the truth only once in our marriage. He said, "Shit happens. The trick is not to step in it. And if you do, for God's sake, June, don't just stand there."

JULIA. It was his fault, Ma.

[MUSIC NO. 19 – EVERYTHING HAPPENS]

He's here and Michael isn't and it's his fault. I want to believe everything happens for a reason, but...

MRS. ADAMS.
NO, NO, NO.
EV'RYTHING HAPPENS
JUST THAT
EV'RYTHING HAPPENS
AN EVENT, OR A DEATH,
A CATASTROPHE
ANY REASON AS TO WHY
IS A REASON YOU SUPPLY
IT JUST HAPPENS
EV'RYTHING HAPPENS
IT'S NOT FATE,
NO GREAT PLAN,
IT'S NOT DESTINY
PUTTING FAITH IN THAT CLICHÉ

GIVES YOUR OWN FREE WILL AWAY
WHEN THINGS HAPPEN
AND THEY WILL HAPPEN
YOU CAN WASTE YOUR WHOLE DAMN LIFE
ASSIGNING BITS OF PHILOSOPHIC MEANING
TO THE FAILURES
AND MISFORTUNES INTERVENING
AND I'LL TELL YOU WHAT YOU GET:
JUST A LIFETIME OF REGRET
NO, NO, NO.
THERE IS NO REASON
FOR WHY EV'RYTHING HAPPENS
IT'S THE CHANGING OF A SEASON,
IT'S A FACT AND IT'S A CONSTANT
AND THE ONLY SANE RESPONSE IS TO ADJUST
NOT TO WISH IT HADN'T HAPPENED
WHEN IT MUST
NOW THE CHURCH WILL TELL YOU ONE THING,
AND YOUR FRIENDS PERHAPS ANOTHER
IF I WERE YOU I'D LISTEN
TO YOUR SLIGHTLY DOTTY MOTHER
WHO LOST OUT ON HER OWN FAIR SHARE
OF GOOD TIMES AND OF LAUGHTER
LISTEN, WHAT MATTERS WHEN THINGS HAPPEN
IS WHAT HAPPENS
AFTER

[MUSIC NO. 19A – AFTER EVERYTHING HAPPENS]

(**MRS. ADAMS** *crosses to exit, patting* **JULIA** *unsentimentally on the shoulder.* **JULIA** *is left alone in the kitchen. The scene begins to shift around her as she reaches for her notebook and a pencil.* **NICK** *appears in isolation playing a bluesy variation on "Everything Happens."* **JOHNNY, DAVY, JIMMY,** *and* **WAYNE** *appear variously in their own time and space. Each one occupies himself in the middle of the night attempting to keep*

*their own desperation at bay by packing for
New York.* **JULIA** *wanders in isolation among
them, considering her mother's advice. The
beginnings of a poem occur to her.)*

Scene Five

> (**JIMMY**, **JOHNNY**, **DAVY**, **NICK**, *and* **WAYNE**
> *disappear as light reveals the front door*
> *of Donny's apartment early the following*
> *morning.* **JULIA**, *in her winter coat, approaches*
> *the door.* **DONNY** *stands in the doorway, still*
> *in his undershirt.* **JULIA** *takes a folded piece*
> *of paper from her coat pocket and hands it to*
> **DONNY**.)

DONNY. *(Apprehensive.)* Your resignation?

JULIA. It's a poem. To you and the guys. There's so much I
didn't see, and I'm so sorry.

DONNY. You don't have to apologize.

> (**DONNY** *opens it and starts to read silently.*)

JULIA. Neither do you. We both know who you're raising
this money for. We're not going to have enough to go
the way you and Michael dreamed, but that's okay.

DONNY. I'm letting him down –

JULIA. You know how Michael and I met? First day of
rehearsal for our high school production of "Desert
Song." I was sulking in the back row 'cause I didn't get
the lead. He plops himself down and says, "Don't sing
because you need to get the lead. Sing because you just
need to sing." And then he says, "The girl who got the
lead stuffs her bra with so much Kleenex, one cigarette
ash and she'll go up like the Hindenburg." That's the
Michael I knew. Sing because you just need to sing.

[MUSIC NO. 20 – WELCOME HOME (PREPRISE)]

> (**JULIA** *exits.* **DONNY** *stands for a moment*
> *watching her disappear into the darkness.*
> *As he reads the poem she has given him, the*
> *outline of a melody begins to take shape.*)

Scene Six

*(**DONNY** remains studying the poem as the light shifts to reveal **NICK**, **JIMMY**, **WAYNE**, **DAVY**, and **JOHNNY**, each in isolation.)*

DAVY. Anyone heard from Donny?

JIMMY. Rehearsal's still on for tonight.

JOHNNY. We can rehearse all we want, but what's the point without Julia?

JIMMY. She's fine. Just a twenty-four-hour bug.

WAYNE. I think they've both got something you don't get over in twenty-four hours.

DAVY. A lotta landmines there.

*(**NICK** crosses to **WAYNE**.)*

NICK. We gotta worry about our next gig falling apart every time they have a spat?

WAYNE. You know, you're a selfish bastard. They deserve all the happiness in the world.

NICK. What is it with you Marines? Always gotta be better than the rest of us. Jesus, it's annoying! And stop picking up my clothes. If I wanted 'em in the drawer, I'd put 'em in the drawer!

*(**NICK**, **WAYNE**, **JIMMY**, **DAVY**, and **JOHNNY** disappear as the scene shifts.)*

Scene Seven

(**DONNY** *is once again alone. Still holding the poem, he begins to sing the words* **JULIA** *has written.*)

DONNY.

NICK LEARNED TO SURVIVE
MEANS YOU NEVER TRUST
ONCE YOU'VE SEEN THE WORST IN MAN, THEN
HOW DO YOU ADJUST?
AND I STAND HERE HELPLESS
MY ARMS EXTENDED
KNOWING FULL WELL, DARLING
YOUR WAR'S NOT ENDED
WELCOME HOME
MY BOYS
WELCOME HOME
MY SONS
WELCOME HOME
MY HUSBAND.
WELCOME HOME
MY LOVE
WELCOME HOME
WELCOME HOME

(*The light shifts to reveal it is late the following afternoon.* **JULIA** *appears and joins* **DONNY** *singing.*)

JULIA & DONNY.

WELCOME

JULIA.

HOME

DONNY. The chorus is a variation on "Taps." See?

JULIA. You didn't have to set it to music.

DONNY. It just came to me.

JULIA. I love it, Donny. But we can't –

DONNY. I know. No one would sit still for this.

JULIA. It wasn't meant for the bandstand. It's about you and the guys. No apologies.

DONNY. But play that in public…

JULIA. It'd be the last time we'd get a booking. We're playing the VA hall tomorrow night. Maybe I can rewrite the words, make it a love song. Something for them. It's still "Welcome Home," but a girl to her fella.

DONNY. Home from the war.

JULIA. Exactly –

DONNY. She's at her door –

JULIA. Yes, and he's coming down the street –

DONNY. Like if Michael had.

JULIA. Well…maybe I'll write it like it might've been.

DONNY. (*Beat.*) I think you should. It's our last show before we have to hitchhike to New York. It'll be perfect.

JULIA. You better put on some coffee. It's gonna be work.

[MUSIC NO. 21 – WELCOME HOME (ROMANTIC)]

(**DONNY** *walks out of the room, leaving* **JULIA** *in isolation as Donny's apartment disappears into the darkness. She studies the manuscript of Donny's music and begins to rework the lyrics of the song aloud.*)

ANY NUMBER OF
WAYS FOR THIS TO GO
FUNNY THING ABOUT THAT IS
THEY SAY, "WRITE WHAT YOU KNOW"
GIRL CAN MEET HER BOY
IT'S AS SIMPLE AS
CAN SHE COME TO TERMS
WITH WHAT SHE HAD AND WHAT SHE HAS?
AND I STAND HERE BREATHLESS,
MY MIND STILL WEIGHING
WHAT MY CHOICES MIGHT BE
AND YET I'M SAYING…

(As the music rises, **JULIA** *imagines the moment of Michael's return to her, as it might have been.)*

Scene Eight

(The scene shifts to the VA hall. **DONNY** *and the rest of the* **BAND** *take their place behind* **JULIA**. *Various* **SERVICEMEN** *enter and mingle and greet one another before taking their seats.* **OLIVER** *arrives and greets several of them,* **MRS. ADAMS** *among them.)*

JULIA.
ALL THE SLEEPLESS NIGHTS
PRAYING YOU'D RETURN
SAFELY TO MY ARMS WITH
ALL THE HONOR YOU WOULD EARN
LETTERS EV'RY DAY
SENT TO REASSURE,
KNOWING ALL THE DANGERS
WERE THE DUTIES OF THE TOUR
NOW OUR WAIT HAS ENDED,
OUR YEARS OF YEARNING
AND I'M AT MY DOORWAY,
MY LOVE RETURNING
"WELCOME HOME,
MY DEAR,
WELCOME HOME,
MY SWEET
WELCOME HOME,
MY HERO
WELCOME HOME,
MY HEART
WELCOME HOME,
WELCOME HOME,
WELCOME HOME"

(The **CROWD** *applauds.* **DONNY** *addresses the crowd from his piano microphone.)*

DONNY. Thank you all very much.

SERVICEMAN 1. You're gonna clean up in New York next week.

DONNY. Thanks.

SERVICEMAN 1. No, thank you. You make us all real proud.

SERVICEMAN 2. We'll all be listening.

(*The* **CROWD** *cheers.*)

DONNY. Well, I gotta tell you when you tune in to the contest, there's no guarantee we'll even be on it.

[MUSIC NO. 21A – OFF TO NEW YORK, FIRST CLASS]

(*There is a concerned murmur from the* **CROWD**.)

See, there's another preliminary NBC's making us go through. How's that for a tribute to the troops? If we make it, they get to claim they have a bunch of genuine American Heroes. I hear Julia sing that word "hero," I wonder who that guy is. I don't know a single one of us that feels like one. That's just a word someone pins on you. I think... Most of the time I just think...

JULIA. (*Genuinely concerned.*) Donny...

DONNY. The wrong guy came home.

(**OLIVER** *rushes the stage and stops him.*)

OLIVER. Hold on, hold on, I think that's enough of the sappy speeches for one night. Besides, that's my department. Who needs NBC when you got Cleveland?

(*Gently singing.*)

HOW 'BOUT A BIG PARADE?
YOU PAID YOUR DUES
AND WE OWE IT TO YA

Listen, for the past few weeks everyone at my club and the Blue Wisp and the Pavilion paid a little extra cover charge. And all the guys here at the V.A. chipped in.

SERVICEMAN 2. Darn right!

(**OLIVER** *hands* **DONNY** *an envelope.*)

OLIVER.

AND NOW YOU GOT IT MADE

From Cleveland with love. Four rooms at the Hotel Astor, reserved and paid for.

*(**OLIVER** reaches into his jacket pocket and pulls out another envelope.)*

And seven tickets on the Cleveland Limited. Pullman Car. First class. Knock 'em dead.

*(The entire **BAND** and **CROWD** cheers as the scene shifts abruptly.)*

Scene Nine

(The **DANCING COUPLES** *cross throughout the space as the center bandstand disappears into the darkness.* **DONNY, JULIA, JIMMY, DAVY, JOHNNY, NICK,** *and* **WAYNE** *step down from the bandstand and make their way to the front of the space which, as the* **DANCING COUPLES** *clear away, appears to be several first-class seats on the train to New York. They take their seats on the train,* **JULIA** *and* **DONNY** *sitting together and the others shifting around like rambunctious schoolboys.)*

[MUSIC NO. 22 – A BAND IN NEW YORK CITY]

JOHNNY.
BUDDY
TAKE THE MOMENT IN
AND REMEMBER HERE AND NOW
AS THE STARTING POINT OF HOW
WE WILL CONQUER NEW YORK CITY

DAVY.
BUDDY
DO YOU REALIZE
WE ARE ON A FIRST-CLASS TRAIN
AND THE WORLD IS OUR DOMAIN
ON THE WAY TO NEW YORK CITY?!

JIMMY.
IT'S THE SAME ASPIRATION
SHARED BY THOUSANDS OF CIVILIANS
IT'S THE MYTHIC LOCATION
WHERE THEY GO TO MAKE THEIR MILLIONS

JULIA & BAND.
SO BROTHER
IT'S THE FANTASY
AND WE'RE LIVING IT IN STYLE
GETTING CLOSER BY THE MILE
ON THE TRAIN TO NEW YORK CITY

TRAIN CONDUCTOR 1.
ROCHESTER!

TRAIN CONDUCTOR 2.
SYRACUSE!

TRAIN CONDUCTOR 3.
SCHENECTADY!

TRAIN CONDUCTOR 4.
ALBANY!

ALL TRAIN CONDUCTORS.
POUGHKEEPSIE!
YONKERS!

JULIA.
DONNY, KID I OWE YOU ONE
NO, I OWE YOU TWO OR THREE!
WITHOUT YOU I WOULD NOT BE

JULIA & ALL TRAIN CONDUCTORS.
PULLING INTO NEW YORK CITY

> (*The scene shifts as a rush of* **NEW YORKERS** *cross the stage. The train seats disappear and when the crowd disperses, elements of a room at the Hotel Astor are assembled.* **DONNY**, **JULIA**, **JIMMY**, **JOHNNY**, *and* **DAVY** *are looking around the room.*)

ENSEMBLE.
PULLIN' INTO NEW YORK

DONNY, JULIA & BAND.
PULLIN' INTO NEW YORK

ENSEMBLE MEN.
UPTOWN VIEWS

ENSEMBLE WOMEN.
THE DAILY NEWS

ENSEMBLE MEN.
WE GOT IT ALL IN NEW YORK

JOHNNY & DAVY.
NEW YORK

NICK, WAYNE & ENSEMBLE MEN.
>IT'S RIGHT THIS WAY

ENSEMBLE WOMEN.
>WELCOME HOME

JOHNNY. That's a hell of a view. I won't sleep with all those lights.

DAVY. This hotel's got bigger beds than I've ever seen in my life!

JOHNNY. You won't be in it – there's a bar downstairs.

>(**NICK** *and* **WAYNE** *rush in from the side.*)

NICK. Is your view better?

JIMMY. We can see down forty-fifth street. But the best is Julia's.

NICK. Let's see it.

JULIA. A lady doesn't let just anyone into her hotel room.

DAVY. Enough hotel rooms, let's see some nightclubs!

DONNY. Just remember, tomorrow's a big day. Don't do anything stupid.

DAVY.
>BROTHER,
>MAKE THE MOST OF IT
>THERE IS ONLY ONE FIRST TIME

JULIA.
>AND TONIGHT'S
>THE FIRST TIME I'M
>ON THE LOOSE
>IN NEW YORK CITY

DONNY. Easy.

JIMMY, JOHNNY, DAVY, NICK & WAYNE.
>IT'S A SPECIAL OCCASION
>THE FULFILLMENT OF A VISION

WAYNE.
>WE SHOULD PLAN OUR INVASION
>WITH OUR MILIT'RY PRECISION

DONNY, JULIA & BAND.
BUDDY, WE'RE UNSTOPPABLE
LIKE A CATCHY GERSHWIN SONG
LIKE THE GIANT APE KING KONG
ON THE TOP OF NEW YORK CITY!

JIMMY.
THEY'VE GOT MORE ART THAN VENICE
BROADWAY SHOWS WITH ETHEL MERMAN!

WAYNE.
AND THE CABS ARE A MENACE
COULD HAVE USED ONE ON A GERMAN

> (**JOHNNY** *spies a gorgeous woman. He pulls* **NICK** *aside.*)

JOHNNY.
BROTHER
GET A LOAD OF THAT
TELL THE OTHERS I GOT LOST

NICK.
BETTER ASK HOW MUCH SHE'LL COST
NUT'N'S FREE IN NEW YORK CITY

BAND & ENSEMBLE MEN.	**JULIA & ENSEMBLE WOMEN.**
YOU'VE GOT CLUBS	BA DO BA DE DO DAT
OVERFLOWIN'	BA DO BA DE DO DAT
WITH	

ALL.
CELEBRITIES AND STARLETS

JULIA & ENSEMBLE WOMEN.	**ENSEMBLE MEN.**
AND HOT HORN SECTIONS	BOM BOM DOO DOO DOO
BLOWING	WAH WAH
AS ARE ALL THE WHORES	
AND HARLOTS	

ALL.
ALL THE RICH AND THE HAUGHTY
(AND THE) ENTOURAGES WITH 'EM
NEED A PLACE TO BE NAUGHTY
AND A BAND TO GIVE 'EM RHYTHM

DONNY, JULIA & BAND.
>WE'RE THAT BAND.

ALL.
>HEAR THAT BAND.
>HEAR THAT BAND.
>
>RIGHT THIS WAY
>RIGHT THIS WAY.

ENSEMBLE MEN.	ENSEMBLE WOMEN.	
DOO DOO DOO DOOT DOO	RIGHT	
DOO DOO DOO DOO	THIS	**JULIA, DONNY & BAND.** BREATHE
DOO DOO DOO DOOT DOO	WAY	
	WE'VE BEEN WAITING	JUST
DOO DOO DOO DOOT DOO	JUST FOR YOU	BREATHE
AND WE HOPE YOU	AND WE HOPE YOU	AND
ENJOY YOUR STAY!	ENJOY YOUR STAY!	ENJOY YOUR STAY!

ALL.
>SO BUDDY
>PUT ME ON THE LIST
>WITH A MILLION OTHER GUYS
>WHO ARE HOPIN' THEY WILL RISE
>TO THE HIGHEST OF THE HEIGHTS
>PLAYING ENDLESS SOLD-OUT NIGHTS
>WITH THE CROWD AT THEIR COMMAND
>ON A TOWERING BANDSTAND
>IN A BAND.
>IN NEW YORK CITY

>**[MUSIC NO. 22A – BAND IN NEW YORK CITY (PLAYOFF)]**

Scene Twelve

(The scene shifts. A door appears, suggesting the corridor of the Hotel Astor, just outside Julia's room.)

JULIA. You still know how to be a gentleman and walk a girl to her door.

DONNY. It's harder than it looks.

JULIA. You're being very respectable.

DONNY. No, I mean that last martini made it harder to walk than it looks.

　　　(Beat.)

What say we all do lunch at the Edison before going to the studio tomorrow.

JULIA. Or Sardi's. I've always wanted to go to Sardi's.

DONNY. That sounds wonderful. Let's do that.

JULIA. *(Beat.)* Well, goodnight.

　　　*(**JULIA** kisses **DONNY** quickly on the cheek. He remains still. She pulls back but not very far at all. **DONNY** slowly moves in to her, turning his head against the side of hers, avoiding a kiss, forcing his hands to stay at his sides.)*

[MUSIC NO. 23 – THIS IS LIFE]

DONNY.
　IF WE WERE IN AN MGM FILM,
　WE WOULD KISS AND WALK
　THROUGH THAT DOOR THERE
　IF WE WERE IN A RADIO PLAY,
　WE'D ADMIT WE'RE FRIENDS
　BUT THERE'S MORE THERE

JULIA.
　IF WE WERE SINGING HAMMERSTEIN SONGS
　WE COULD FIX ALL THE WRONGS IN RHYME
　BUT THIS IS LIFE,
　WITH THE HEARTACHE IT BRINGS
　AND WE KNOW THAT THESE THINGS TAKE TIME

DONNY.

> IF WE WERE IN A HEMINGWAY BOOK,
> WE WOULD LAUGH AND DRINK
> TILL THE MORNING
> IF THIS WERE A BALLET, THEN I MIGHT
> SWEEP YOU OFF YOUR FEET
> WITHOUT WARNING

JULIA.

> OR FILM NOIR WITH A DANG'ROUS AFFAIR
> I WOULD ASK IF YOU'D CARE TO STAY
> BUT THIS IS LIFE,
> AND I'M WONDERING IF
> WE SHOULD PLAY IT A DIFF'RENT WAY

DONNY.

> MAYBE PERFECT NIGHTS OF CELEBRATION

JULIA.

> HOTEL HALLWAY BRIEF FLIRTATION
> MIGHT BE OVERRATED

JULIA & DONNY.

> LIFE'S MORE COMPLICATED

DONNY.

> WE COULD WRITE OUR OWN
> TAKE ON IT

JULIA.

> OR LEAVE WELL ENOUGH ALONE
> SHAKE ON IT

DONNY.

> SHAKE ON IT
> NO ONE PLANNED FOR A MOMENT LIKE THIS,
> THERE'S NO PERFECT SCRIPT
> THAT PROVIDES US
> WORDS TO SAY, OR THE ANSWERS THAT MIGHT
> OVERCOME THE PAST THAT DIVIDES US

JULIA.

> MOVIE STARS WITH THE PASSIONS THEY FEEL
> SOMEHOW IN THE LAST REEL
> UNITE

DONNY.

THAT'S RIGHT

DONNY & JULIA.

BUT THIS IS LIFE,

SO AT LEAST FOR TODAY

WE SHOULD PROBABLY SAY GOODNIGHT

*(***DONNY*** steps away from* **JULIA.** *She watches him walk away before turning toward the door, opening it, and walking inside. The door closes behind her and the scene shifts.)*

[MUSIC NO. 23A – CHICAGO FOUR PLAY]

Scene Thirteen

(The door to the hotel room disappears into the darkness as the piano and drum set appear center. Members of the **CHICAGO FOUR BAND**, *the band representing Illinois, are playing the final notes of their preliminary audition in the NBC Studio rehearsal room. A folding table appears at the edge of the space.* **JAMES HAUPT**, *the middle-aged director of the broadcast, and* **ANDRE BARUCH**, *the host, are at the table. An officious but kind female* **PRODUCTION ASSISTANT** *stands to the side, clipboard in hand.)*

JAMES HAUPT. Well done, fellas, well done.

(The members of the **CHICAGO FOUR BAND** *begin to take their instruments and make their way out of the room.)*

We'll be letting you know by tomorrow night.

PRODUCTION ASSISTANT. Says here you're at the Plaza, correct?

*(***TOM**, *the trumpet player for the Chicago Four Band, approaches the* **PRODUCTION ASSISTANT**.*)*

TOM. That's right.

JAMES HAUPT. Paula, could you have the next band start setting up?

PRODUCTION ASSISTANT. Absolutely.

(Crossing to the edge of the space and calling off.) The Donny Nova Band. Donny Nova Band please. We're ready for you. Go ahead and take your places.

(The **CHICAGO FOUR BAND** *follows her to exit.* **DONNY**, **JULIA**, *and the* **BAND** *begin entering the studio, crossing paths with the exiting* **CHICAGO FOUR BAND**.*)*

JIMMY. Thank you so much.

NICK. *(Passing* **TOM.***)* Tom? It's Nick Radel!

TOM. Nick! Well how are you old sport?

NICK. Did you fellas make it? Are you in?

TOM. We find out tomorrow. Tell you what, you root for Illinois and we'll root for Ohio and we'll both make it to Sunday.

NICK. Deal.

TOM. We should have lunch tomorrow. I'm at the Plaza. Ring over.

NICK. How 'bout you ring me. I'm at the Astor. So good to see you.

    *(***TOM** *exits with his band.)*

    (Aside to **WAYNE.***)* Stuck-up prick.

    *(***NICK** *hurries to take his place in the center of the studio with* **DONNY** *and the* **BAND.***)*

PRODUCTION ASSISTANT. This is the Donny Nova Band featuring Julia Trojan.

JAMES HAUPT. How do you do.

PRODUCTION ASSISTANT. Here we have our director James Haupt, and of course the program's host, Andre Baruch.

DONNY. An honor to meet you.

JAMES HAUPT. What's the name of your tune, son?

DONNY. "Love Will Come and Find Me Again." Music by me, and the lyrics by Julia here.

JAMES HAUPT. Now listen, we're running behind so just give us a verse, chorus out, or chorus, bridge, chorus out, whichever.

DONNY. Sure thing.

    (To the **BAND.***)* Guys, just last chorus to the end.

JAMES HAUPT. Go ahead whenever you're ready.

[MUSIC NO. 24 – LOVE WILL COME (AUDITION)]

DONNY. *(Spoken in rhythm.)* Two, three!

JULIA.

> TROUBLE IS THE MORE YOU DENY,
> THE MORE YOU DON'T EVEN TRY,
> THE MORE THE WORLD PASSES BY IN A HAZE
> SOON YOU FIND YOU DON'T EVEN KNOW
> HOW MANY YEARS YOU LET GO,
> THE CHANCES WASTED IN SO MANY WAYS

JAMES HAUPT. Hey guys, I'm sorry to stop you. That's great. That's good. That's a fine voice you have there, miss.

JULIA. Thank you.

JAMES HAUPT. And it's a really terrific tune.

DONNY. Thanks.

JAMES HAUPT. Look, it says here you're all veterans, is that true?

DONNY. Yes, Sir.

JAMES HAUPT. All just back?

DONNY, DAVY & WAYNE. Yes, Sir.

JAMES HAUPT. And the young lady?

JULIA. My husband was in the Thirty-seventh Infantry. He died in battle.

JAMES HAUPT. My condolences, Ma'am.

JULIA. Thank you.

JAMES HAUPT. This is a story folks can really get behind. We want you in the broadcast and because of the military angle, we're putting you up last. The finale.

DONNY. Oh, Mr. Haupt, thank you so much.

JULIA. You really mean it?

JAMES HAUPT. Yes, Ma'am.

JIMMY, JOHNNY, DAVY, NICK & WAYNE. *(Variously.)* Thanks so much – This is just swell – I can't believe it.

JAMES HAUPT. Paula, go ahead and have them sign the release forms now – put us ahead on Sunday.

PRODUCTION ASSISTANT. Now, these forms are the releases that allow us to broadcast your song. The name of the song is "Love Will Come and Find Me Again" and you two are the sole composer and lyricist?

DONNY & JULIA. Yes, Ma'am.

(The **PRODUCTION ASSISTANT** *writes in the title on the form.)*

PRODUCTION ASSISTANT. Very well, then sign here. Both of you. We'll see you Sunday at the Palace Theatre. Use the stage door on forty-seventh street. This is your copy. Congratulations.

*(***DONNY** *and* **JULIA** *sign as the rest of the* **BAND** *are making their way out of the space.)*

DONNY. Thanks so much. So long, Gentlemen.

*(***DONNY***,* **JULIA***, and the* **BAND** *exit.)*

JAMES HAUPT. Okay, who's next?

PRODUCTION ASSISTANT. We're up to Texas. "The Boogie Woogie Wranglers."

JAMES HAUPT. Jesus Christ. Damn good thing we're sponsored by Aspirin.

[MUSIC NO. 24A – INTO THE BIG BROADCAST]

(The scene begins to shift as the various **STAGE TECHNICIANS***,* **PRODUCTION ASSISTANTS***, and* **RIVAL BAND MEMBERS** *begin to cross throughout the space.)*

Scene Fourteen

> *(The folding table and chairs of the NBC Studios rehearsal room are rearranged as other elements of the backstage wing of the Palace Theatre appear. Music from a band playing onstage can be heard as the live broadcast is nearing its big finale.* **DAVY** *and* **NICK** *appear.)*

DAVY. Do you see him?

NICK. No.

> *(The* **PRODUCTION ASSISTANT** *rushes past them.)*

PRODUCTION ASSISTANT. Please don't wait in the wings. Only the next band up should be out here.

NICK. We're the next after the next.

PRODUCTION ASSISTANT. Just please keep this area clear.

> *(The* **PRODUCTION ASSISTANT** *rushes off.* **DONNY** *and* **JULIA** *enter and cross to* **DAVY** *and* **NICK**.)*

DONNY. We checked all the other dressing rooms. He's not here.

JULIA. I don't understand it. What did he say after the microphone check?

DONNY. Just that he needed to take care of some things but he'd be back by showtime.

> *(**WAYNE** *and* **JOHNNY** *rush in, followed by* **JIMMY**.)*

WAYNE. We got him, he's here.

DONNY. Jesus, Jimmy! What the hell are you trying to pull?!

JIMMY. I'm sorry, but you gotta see this.

JULIA. Where were you? We were worried sick!

JIMMY. The New York Public Library. Law section.

NICK. Aw, for God's sake!

DONNY. We're on in two more numbers!

JIMMY. Donny, listen! You should have shown me this form earlier.

> (**JIMMY** *pulls the release form from his coat pocket.*)

Look. This clause right here. It's the underlying rights to your song.

DONNY. What's that?

JIMMY. You signed away the rights to your song. And this clause right here: they're only obligated to use us as walk-ons.

DONNY. What?

JOHNNY. I don't get it.

JIMMY. It means if we go out there, NBC and MGM own your song outright and they can have Frank Sinatra or anybody else sing it in the picture while we fake playing along in the background like a bunch of monkeys.

DONNY. No –

JIMMY. And if you ever want to perform the song again yourself, you pay *them* royalties to do it.

DONNY. Did all these bands have to sign that thing?

JIMMY. They must have, but I don't think they understand what they've signed. That's what they're counting on.

JULIA. What are we going to do?

JIMMY. You can't just give away your song. You can't go out there.

DONNY. God dammit!

NICK. I say walk away, Donny.

DAVY. You can say, "I came, I saw, I said fuck it."

WAYNE. I'm with them. Let's just go. Screw these people. All they want to do is use our uniforms and wave us around like flags. We're not props, Donny. We're not for sale. We've already given them everything we got. We're goddamn United States veterans, and these people wouldn't know real sacrifice if it slapped 'em in the face.

DONNY. *(Beat.)* That's exactly what we gotta do. Slap 'em in the face. Julia, do you know all the original words you wrote for "Welcome Home"?

JULIA. Yes.

DONNY. And you could sing them right now?

JULIA. Donny, I don't –

DONNY. Can you sing every original word you wrote or not?

JULIA. Yes.

DONNY. If we go out there, we gotta play something they wouldn't *dare* put in a movie. Something Frank Sinatra or Bing Crosby wouldn't have the balls to sing. In five minutes we could be in every living room in America. Let's tell 'em the truth. Let 'em all hear what we go through every goddamn day. Let the guys who made it home know somebody out there has their backs. "Welcome Home."

[MUSIC NO. 24B – THIS IS LIFE (REPRISE)]

JOHNNY. You're talking about a suicide mission.

WAYNE. *(Resolved.)* Blow it up.

DAVY. Yeah, blow it up.

JULIA. Donny, are you sure? We could be blacklisted, or worse.

DONNY. We've all been through worse.

THIS IS NO NAIVE HOLLYWOOD DREAM
IT'S A GUTSY RISK
WE'LL BE TAKING
TIMES LIKE THIS,
YOU HOLD ON TO WHAT'S REAL
THAT'S THE HONEST STATEMENT
WE'RE MAKING
I'LL MARCH BACK INTO BATTLE ONCE MORE
IF I'M FIGHTING IT FOR WHAT'S TRUE

What happened over there is true.

What this band means to all of us is true. What I feel for you, Julia, is true. No matter how tough it is, no matter how much time it takes, I need to be with you. *That* is true.

'CAUSE THIS IS LIFE
WITH THE CRAZINESS OF,
THE REALITY OF,
THE NECESSITY OF,
BEING MADLY IN LOVE WITH YOU

(*JULIA kisses **DONNY** passionately as the scene shifts abruptly.*)

[MUSIC NO. 24C – ANDRE'S FINAL INTRO]

(**ANDRE BARUCH** *appears before an NBC microphone as the stage of the Palace Theatre assembles and the live broadcast continues. A show curtain has descended, behind which the main bandstand awaits. **JULIA**, **DONNY**, and the **BAND** begin to take their places, instruments in hand, on the bandstand as **ANDRE BARUCH** speaks.*)

ANDRE BARUCH. Our final group of the evening hails from the great state of Ohio, featuring a band of heroes representing the Army, the Navy, and the Marines – yes, folks, each and every one of them triumphantly back from the war. And wouldn't you know, their soloist is a young lady who carries her gold star as proudly as anyone could. She sings tonight from heartbreaking experience, a song called "Love Will Come and Find Me Again." I'm sure everyone listening joins me in the certainty that her brave fallen soldier up there will hear her every word. So without further ado, I invite you all to welcome to the stage, the Donny Nova Band featuring Julia Trojan.

(**ANDRE BARUCH** *exits and applause is heard. The show curtain rises on the bandstand. There is a moment of silence as **DONNY**, **JULIA**, and the **BAND** silently acknowledge one another and what they are about to do.*

> DONNY *holds the silence – the "dead air" –*
> *even longer, staring out at the audience and*
> *the contest personnel, defying them to do*
> *anything about it. Then* DONNY *begins...)*

DONNY. Okay, Johnny.

[MUSIC NO. 25 – WELCOME HOME – FINALE]

> (JOHNNY *plays a hot swing pattern on his*
> *high hat.)*

Faster.

> (JOHNNY *pushes the tempo.)*

Faster.

> (JOHNNY *pushes it even faster.)*

Faster!

> (JOHNNY *pushes it again to a blazing tempo.*
> DONNY *adds the first piano pattern. He*
> *beams at* JULIA.*)*

Now, sing.

JULIA.

JOHNNY MADE IT HOME
MOST OF HIM AT LEAST
HAD THREE OPERATIONS
BUT THE PAIN HAS NOT DECREASED
NICK LEARNED TO SURVIVE
MEANS YOU NEVER TRUST
ONCE YOU'VE SEEN THE WORST IN MAN, THEN
HOW DO YOU ADJUST?

DAVY CRACKS A JOKE,
CLAIMS TO BE ALRIGHT
DRINKS A FIFTH OF VODKA
IN HIS KITCHEN EV'RY NIGHT
AND I STAND HERE TRYING
LIKE MOTHER MARY,
WITH MY PRIVATE BURDEN
OF GRIEF TO CARRY

WELCOME HOME
MY BOYS,
WELCOME HOME
MY SONS,
WELCOME HOME
MY HUSBAND,
WELCOME HOME
MY LOVE
WELCOME HOME,
WELCOME HOME,
WELCOME HOME

WAYNE IS NEVER FREE
SCHEDULES OUT HIS DAY
FILLING EV'RY MINUTE
JUST TO KEEP THE GHOSTS AWAY
HE COULD NEVER GET
BACK THE LIFE HE HAD
FACED WITH RAISING KIDS
WHO DID NOT RECOGNIZE THEIR DAD

JIMMY MADE IT BACK TO TOWN
FOUR MONTHS AGO
LIVED TO TELL OF THINGS
NO ONE COULD BEAR TO KNOW
KEEPS HIS GUARD UP NOW,
A LOT GOES UNDISCUSSED
FOCUSES ON FIGHTING
WHAT HE FINDS UNJUST

WELCOME HOME
MY BOYS,
WELCOME HOME
MY SONS,
WELCOME HOME
MY HUSBAND,
WELCOME HOME
MY LOVE
WELCOME HOME,
WELCOME HOME,
WELCOME HOME

DONNY DOES HIS BEST
TRYING TO PRETEND
WHAT HE DOESN'T TALK ABOUT
WON'T MATTER IN THE END
DONNY MADE IT HOME
BUT THINKS IT WASN'T FAIR
HOW HE MADE IT OUT
BUT LEFT HIS BUDDY THERE
DONNY DOESN'T SLEEP
BECAUSE THE NIGHTMARES COME
DONNY WANTS AN ANSWER,
DONNY LOOKS FOR ABSOLUTION
AND I'D GIVE UP ANYTHING
IF I COULD GIVE HIM SOME

AND I STAND HERE HELPLESS,
MY ARMS EXTENDED
KNOWING FULL WELL DARLING
YOUR WAR'S NOT ENDED

WELCOME HOME
WELCOME HOME
MY HUSBAND,
WELCOME HOME
MY LOVE,
WELCOME HOME,
WELCOME HOME,
WELCOME HOME
MY BOYS,
WELCOME HOME
MY SONS,
WELCOME HOME
MY HUSBAND,
WELCOME HOME
MY LOVE
WELCOME HOME,
WELCOME HOME,
WELCOME HOME

> *(They finish the number in near collapse.*
> **DONNY** *rises from the piano and embraces*

JULIA, *comforting her.* **ANDRE BARUCH** *enters and takes his place at the microphone. The show curtain descends, obscuring the bandstand.)*

[MUSIC NO. 25A – AND THE WINNER REALLY IS]

ANDRE BARUCH. The Donny Nova Band, Ladies and Gentlemen. What an extraordinary evening of *surprises* this has been. Our director this evening has been James Haupt and here he comes now with the judges' decision on which song and its talented creators will be featured in a brand new MGM motion picture musical.

> *(***JAMES HAUPT*** enters and hands ***ANDRE BARUCH*** a card.)*

Thank you, James. Ladies and Gentlemen, the winner of the Bayer Aspirin American Songbook of Popular Music Tribute to the Troops Song Competition is...

> *(There is a drum roll, then a brassy fanfare as the entire space is flooded with light. The fanfare rises in volume. The show curtain disappears to reveal the front facade of a movie palace on a New York street. The building's marquee announces "Frank Sinatra and June Havoc in MGM's Musical Spectacular* The Boys Are Back.*)*

Scene Fifteen

(The doors to the cinema swing open and **DONNY**, **JULIA**, **JIMMY**, **DAVY**, **JOHNNY**, **NICK**, *and* **WAYNE** *walk out onto the sidewalk. The faint sound of the movie soundtrack can be heard from within.* **DONNY**, **JULIA**, *and the* **BAND** *stare blankly up at the marquee before them.* **DAVY** *holds a box of popcorn. His munching on its contents is the only sound the group seems to be able to make.)*

JIMMY. *(Long, suspenseful beat.)* Hard to believe it's up on the big screen.

DONNY. Sinatra sounded just like I thought he would.

DAVY. No one's gonna see this turkey.

JULIA. *(Beat.)* Congratulations, Illinois.

WAYNE. Bravo, Chicago.

NICK. Stuck-up pricks.

JOHNNY. And I thought we were the losers.

(A young and pretty bobby-soxer, **BETSY**, *walks out of the cinema doors.)*

BETSY. Excuse me, Mr. Nova, Miss Trojan. I'm awfully sorry to bother you, but could I have your autographs?

*(**BETSY** extends a small autograph book and pen.)*

JULIA. Sure thing.

DONNY. What's your name?

BETSY. Betsy. I recognized you in there before the lights went down.

JULIA. I hope you don't think we're rude leaving before the end.

BETSY. Not at all. It's a real stinker.

I have your newest record. Oh, and I just love your voice Miss Trojan.

JULIA. Thank you.

BETSY. I'll be at your concert at the Rainbow Room tomorrow night, you know.

DONNY. So folks here in New York let their kids go out on the town alone?

(**DONNY** *hands* **BETSY**'s *book back to her.*)

BETSY. Oh, no, they're coming with me. They love you just as much as I do.

DONNY. Ain't that swell.

BETSY. You know, me and my family'll never forget hearing you on that contest last year. It changed our lives. So thank you. My father served.

DONNY. Give me that back.

[MUSIC NO. 25B – EPILOGUE]

(**DONNY** *motions for the autograph book and* **BETSY** *nervously hands it back.* **DONNY** *scribbles something more into it and hands it back to her.*)

Show that to someone at the door tomorrow night. They'll take you and your family backstage. We'd like to meet him.

BETSY. Yes, sir.

(**BETSY** *exits excitedly.*)

DONNY. *(Teasingly.)*
BOBBY-SOXERS SWOON AT MY CHARMS

(**NICK** *playfully smacks the back of* **DONNY**'s *head.*)

JULIA. Oh, give me a break.

DONNY. *(Genuinely.)*
BACKED UP BY MY BROTHERS IN ARMS

(*A group of* **PASSERSBY** *enters and notices* **DONNY**, **JULIA**, *and the* **BAND**. *A* **YOUNG WOMAN** *in the group points excitedly.*)

YOUNG WOMAN. It *is* them. It's the Donny Nova Band!

WAYNE. *(Anxiously.)* Oh, no...

> *(The group of* **PASSERSBY** *surround* **DONNY**, **JULIA**, *and the* **BAND**. *Another group of* **PASSERSBY** *enters and joins the excitement of seeing the celebrities. Camera flashbulbs begin to go off. Pens and paper are brandished for more autographs. Even more* **PASSERSBY** *enter and* **DONNY**, **JULIA**, *and the* **BAND** *disappear behind a growing mob of adulation. A strobe storm of flashbulbs goes off. The facade of the movie palace and its marquee disappear. The sound of the cheering crowd rises as* **DONNY**, **JULIA**, *and the* **BAND** *are now seen on tour.)*

VOICE-OVER RADIO ANNOUNCER. Chicago's Chez Paris Nightclub is proud to present the kick-off engagement for the nationwide tour of the boys, and *girl*, that have captured America's hearts! Direct from their sold-out run at the world-famous Rainbow Room in New York, it's the Donny Nova Band!

DONNY & JULIA.

> SO GET OUTTA MY WAY!
> FIND SOMEBODY ELSE
> WHO GIVES A FIG WHAT YOU SAY
> GO DISCIPLINE SOMEONE OTHER
> LAST TIME I CHECKED
> YOU WERE NOT MY MOTHER!

DONNY. Hello Atlanta! We love your Southern hospitality.

JULIA. Philadelphia, you do show love for your brothers!

> *(The scene shifts to Oliver's Nightclub. There is a packed house and* **MRS. ADAMS** *is comfortably by* **OLIVER**'s *side.)*

OLIVER. I keep tellin' 'em to go play someplace else, but they just keep comin' back. Cleveland welcomes home the Donny Nova Band –

MRS. ADAMS. Featuring Julia Trojan!

DONNY, JULIA, MRS. ADAMS, BAND & FULL ENSEMBLE.
YOU KNOW WHO TELLS ME "STOP"?
YOU KNOW WHO TELLS ME
"YOU DON'T HAVE WHAT IT TAKES
AND YOU WILL NEVER REACH THE TOP"?
YOU KNOW WHO TELLS ME "STOP"?
NO, NO, NO
NO, NO
NO-BODY
(Blackout.)

End of Play

[MUSIC NO. 26 – BOWS & EXIT MUSIC]